"All right, whoever you are, I've got a cleaver and I'm not afraid to use it," the guy said.

He tiptoed toward us. There was nothing we could do. We were totally and utterly trapped. Biff and I huddled close together, and I swear I could hear *her* pulse racing. My knee continued to throb, but I barely noticed it through all of the paralyzing fear. I saw his black hiking boots, moist and laced with salt from melted snow, just seconds before his face appeared, hovering over us. My jaw dropped so fast I think It popped. The incredible green eyes staring down at us widened.

"Jane?"

And looking down at me right then . . . was Hot Connor.

Also by Emma Harrison

EMMA HARRISON

Tourist Trap

Is he a summer fling
or the real thing?

The Best Girl

EMMA HARRISON

HARPER TEEN

An Imprint of **HarperCollins***Publishers*

Acknowledgments
Special thanks to Amanda Maciel, with whom
I hope to keep working for a long time!

HarperTeen is an imprint of HarperCollins Publishers.

The Best Girl
Copyright © 2008 by Emma Harrison
All rights reserved. Printed in the United States of America.
No part of this book may be used or reproduced in any manner
whatsoever without written permission except in the case of brief
quotations embodied in critical articles and reviews. For information
address HarperCollins Children's Books, a division of HarperCollins
Publishers, 1350 Avenue of the Americas, New York, NY 10019.
www.harperteen.com

Library of Congress Catalog Card Number: 2007929095
ISBN 978-0-06-122824-7

Typography by Andrea Vandergrift
❖
First Edition

For my sister,
my "Best Girl,"
with love

Chapter 1

This is it. You're almost done, I told myself as a cold gust of wind nearly knocked me into an evergreen. *One more exam and you're home free. Well, not exactly* home, *but still. No studying for four whole weeks.*

My very fingertips tingled in anticipation—or was that from the frigid cold? Either way, I couldn't believe I was on my way to my last final of my first semester of freshman year. It was almost over. The week I had dreaded ever since midterms. And it hadn't even been that bad.

Sure, I'd spent countless hours on a hard-as-granite chair in the library, surrounded by highlighted textbooks and nursing a rank case of permanent coffee breath. And of course there were half a dozen moments when my mind had gone utterly blank and I couldn't even remember how to spell my own name, let alone who had written *The Beauty Myth* or why.

1

But at least I hadn't been in it alone. Everywhere I had looked for the past week, there had been fresh stress-zits, mismatched clothing, looks of abject confusion. People who had never spoken to each other before huddled over notebooks and calculators and art history slides, helping to cram each other's heads with as much information as possible. It had been sort of cool, the way everyone had come together. And now, as I rushed over the frozen brick walks of Colorado University, I checked out the happy faces of the kids who were already done, already free, laughing as they loaded their suitcases and laundry bags into their parents' cars.

Good for you, I thought. *In less than two hours, I'll be right there with you.*

Except that I wouldn't be quite so carefree and happy. Because unlike all those kids who were looking forward to four weeks of home-cooked meals, day-long naps, and having their laundry folded for them by loving mothers, I was not going home. I was going to hell. Perhaps I should take my time on this last test.

I turned the corner at the Science Building and was hit in the face with another shock of cold wind. With one swift and practiced motion, I pulled my knit cap lower and my wool scarf higher so that only the slits of my eyes were visible. Everyone had told me I'd get used to the frigid mountain winter. It had yet to happen.

Okay, Farrah, forget about tomorrow. One thing at a time. Just get through this exam, I told myself.

But I couldn't help it. As my eyes blurred from the wind, my mind drifted to this afternoon and my bus ride to Vail. To all the insanity that would await me there. I still had not wrapped my brain around the fact that my brother, Jonah, was getting married, let alone that it was happening in less than two weeks. And he wasn't just tying the knot, he was tying the knot with one of the wealthiest socialites in all of America. My former Deadhead brother was marrying Marni Shay, daughter of Brendan Shay, the most successful preppy clothing designer of the last decade. Successful enough to rival Ralph Lauren and Tommy Hilfiger. This wedding wasn't just going to be extravagant. It was going to be a million-dollar affair attended by fashionistas, politicians, old-guard Hollywood, young starlets, and trust-fund babies. Which not only meant that I was going to feel like a troll by comparison for the next few weeks (you try standing next to cover models and not feeling Orc-ish), but my mother was going to be one big ball of stress. And that was never fun.

Why couldn't Jonah and Marni have just eloped to Barbados? Then I wouldn't have to be the "best man." (Marni wanted a traditional wedding, but did grant my brother the concession of having a female—me—stand by his side as he read his vows.) If they eloped, I wouldn't have to wear that ridiculous ball gown and give a speech in front of all those people and . . . God. Maybe *I* should just hop a plane to Barbados. The sun, the sand, the *warmth* . . . ah, the warmth . . .

"Watch out!"

In my frigid state of daydream, it took me way too long to react to the warning. All I saw was a red scarf, a muddy tire, and a green book bag coming at me way too fast. I was about to get creamed, and all my brain registered was: *Well, guess I won't have to wear that gown after all.*

I braced myself. The bike skidded and toppled. Half a dozen books went flying. Someone was lying on the ground. The wind whistled. Was I dead? Had I hit my head? Was I bleeding? I looked down and found that I hadn't even moved. It was over and I was unscathed.

"Oh my God!" I cried, recovering myself. "Are you all right?"

The biker pushed himself up and glanced at a scrape on his bare right leg. Yeah, he was wearing shorts. A lot of these masochistic Coloradans wore shorts even when it was below freezing. I wasn't sure if they were tough or just stupid.

"Nothing a brief hospital stay won't fix," he joked.

Oh, no way. I knew that voice. He finally lifted his face, and my eyes widened.

Hot Connor. It was actually Hot Connor. So nicknamed by myself and my roommate, Dana, to distinguish him from Creepy Connor and Dumb Connor, two Connors on our floor in the dorm, who could not hope to exist on the same gorgeousness plane as Hot Connor. His last name was Davy and he was in my English Literature class and I had been crushing on him since the very first day when he'd walked in with his perfectly disheveled blond hair, Oakley sunglasses, and mango-banana smoothie. I had been *lusting* after him ever since he'd opened his mouth to defend the view that Jane Austen was a feminist ahead of her time. Now *that's* hot. Also? Those Oakleys had been hiding the most stunning green eyes of all time. I mean, take-your-breath-right-out-of-you stunning. Eyes that were now focused on me.

"Are *you* all right?" he asked. He was bleeding and I had caused it and *he* was asking *me* if I was all right.

"Uh . . . shyuh-huh," I said, turning "sure" into "uh-huh" mid-thought. "Sorry about that. I . . . didn't see you."

"My fault," he said, swiping at his scrape with a crumpled napkin he'd produced from his backpack. "I just finished my last final and I think I'm giddy with freedom."

"I'm . . . I'm . . ." I wasn't sure what I was trying to say. Pretty much anything to keep him there, I guess. I mean, I'd dreamed of talking to him the entire semester. Although in those dreams I was always a lot more coherent than this. And also he had been shirtless. They were, after all, dreams.

"Oh, hey. You're Jane, right? Jane Morris." He reached over, hooked his finger over my scarf, and pulled it down to see my face better. "Yep. It's you."

Suddenly I was sweating and blushing and no longer felt the cold, though I hoped he assumed the redness in my face came from only the wind. I could not believe he knew my name. Well, my middle name anyway. I had been using "Jane" ever since I'd arrived at school. I figured college was giving me a chance to reinvent myself and the first thing to go was my awful first name. Do you know how many people have laughed when they realized my mother named me after one of Charlie's Angels? And the one who went totally batty later in life, no less? Too many.

"Yeah, that's Jane. I mean . . . I'm me. I mean. That's me. Jane is me."

I had to be having a stress-induced, psychotic break. There was no way Hot Connor really knew who I was.

"Wow. Finals week really did a number on your brain, huh?" he joked.

I laughed through my mortification. "I still have one more," I managed to say. Though at the moment Ancient Civilizations seemed mighty unimportant.

"Well, I'm glad you're all right," Hot Connor said, reaching down to pick up his mountain bike. "I wouldn't want to be responsible for maiming the reporter who single-handedly forced the dining hall to buy new frozen yogurt machines. That was the greatest moment of my life."

"You read my article?" I asked.

"I make it a point to read the school paper cover to cover. I like to be informed," he said with mock seriousness.

"It is a highly respected outlet for information," I joked back.

This was a universal and ongoing joke at school.

Our student-run paper, *The Chronicle*, was actually completely lame. For example, my groundbreaking yogurt machine story had made the front page. Still, it would look good on my résumé when I graduated.

"Seriously, though, I always look for your byline," Connor told me. "You're one of the only competent writers at that rag."

"Th . . . thanks," I said.

Not only did he know who I was, he appreciated my writing! When was my alarm going to go off already and wake me up from this dream?

Hot Connor looked at his heavy-duty sports watch. "You'd better get going. You don't want to miss your last test, and I am going to be late for work. Have a good break, Jane."

I wanted to say something cool. Something so stunningly clever he would think about it all through break and search me out the second we returned just because he wanted to be around a girl who thought so very fast on her feet. But all I could think to say was,"Later!"

I'm not even sure if he heard me, because he had already straddled his bike and taken off. I took a deep breath and sighed, watching the steam from my breath dance in the wind. Well, at least he'd given me something to fantasize about for the next few weeks while I was in wedding hell. I'd take what I could get.

"It's not that I don't like Marni herself. I mean, she can be fun and sweet and all," I told Dana as the elevator opened on the bottom floor. The dorm was eerily deserted since we were two of the last people to leave. "It's just that I don't like everything she stands for. The premium on outward beauty, the focusing on superficial things . . ."

"The stealing of your brother-slash-best friend?" Dana said, leveling me with a knowing stare.

"She's not stealing my brother," I said, even as a cold fist of fear gripped my heart. Because Dana was right, of course. I was scared to death of losing Jonah. Up until my brother's engagement, he and I had been best friends—either talking or texting at least once a day. Once the wedding planning had started, our contact had gradually petered off until now we were down to about once a week. That was unacceptable to me. My brother was about the only stable, normal person in my life. I couldn't handle the idea that I might be losing him.

"Look, you just have to try to remember that your brother is doing what makes him happy," Dana said, pausing in the center of the sunlit lobby.

"And yeah, things are gonna change. He's got a whole new family to deal with. But I happen to think Jonah's a good guy. And that means he's not gonna forget about you."

"Ya think?" I asked.

"I think."

My Nike watch beeped and I checked the time. It was already noon. "Crap. I'm gonna have to motor if I'm gonna make my bus."

"Yeah, and my mom's waiting by the curb. So hug me now," Dana said, reaching up.

We hugged quickly. I shoved open the door and stopped in my tracks. There were a few SUVs and mom-car sedans waiting at the curb, but right at the end of the walk was a gleaming stretch limo. A driver in a suit stood outside the door holding a sign that read, F. J. MORRIS.

"F. J. Morris? That doesn't mean you, does it?" Dana asked.

Dana was the only person at school, aside from my floor monitor, who knew my real first name—since it had been on her original housing letter and all. Of course F. J. Morris was me. We both knew it. But we were both too confused to accept it. The driver, a handsome, middle-aged Native American man with long dark hair, stepped forward.

"Ms. Morris?" he asked.

"How did you know?" I asked.

"Your brother described you for me," he said with a smile. "He was dead-on."

Ah. So he told you to look for the flat-chested, freckle-face with the huge head of curly red hair?

"I'm here to give you a ride to the River Lodge, compliments of the Shay family," he said, taking the bags right off my shoulders as he tucked the sign underneath his arm.

I eyed the limousine's tinted windows warily. "My mother's not in there, is she?" Because if she was, I was not ready for it. I'd rather take the bus.

The driver laughed and took the garment bag, holding it up effortlessly so that it wouldn't trail on the salt-and-Ice Melt–covered walk.

"No, Miss," he said.

"Well, okay then," I told him, clapping my mittened hands together. I turned to Dana. "I guess my limo has arrived."

Dana narrowed her eyes. "Well. Looks like someone's warming up to the idea of this wedding."

I laughed as my driver opened the door for me. "Not quite," I said. "But *this* I can get on board with."

I stared out the window of the limousine, trying to appreciate the beauty of the landscape as it scrolled by. The snow-topped peaks, the tall evergreens, the wispy white clouds high in the blue sky. I tried not to feel nervous about the place I was being whisked away to. Tried not to feel like there was no way I was going to fit in. I hated this feeling. This creepy doubt that started in my stomach and snaked out to cover my heart.

For the last few months at school, I had been exactly who I wanted to be. Jane Morris, intrepid reporter and member of the club cross-country team. Jane was a hard worker, a wearer of baggy sweaters and little to no makeup. Jane was a good friend—the person you could always count on to walk you home from a party if you were too drunk to make it yourself, or tell off the guy who had ditched you to play the new Madden Football all night long with his buddies. Jane Morris was cool. She was confident (unless Hot Connor was talking to her). She was smart and spoke her mind. I liked Jane Morris. I just had this awful feeling that she was going to evaporate the second she got around her mother and all those fashion-plate socialites. That she would feel less-than. And Farrah Morris—who had felt less-than most of her life— would come back with a vengeance.

"Everything okay back there?" the driver asked, glancing in the rearview mirror.

"Yeah. Why?" I asked, startled.

"It's just you've been letting out these sort of tortured sighs every few minutes," he told me. "If you don't mind me noticing."

"I have?" I laughed quietly. "Who knew?"

Just then the tight road opened up onto a circular drive and River Lodge loomed before us. My jaw dropped and I fell toward the window to take it all in. The main building was a tremendous log structure with thousands of huge, gleaming windows affording views of the mountains from all angles. The gingerbread eaves were peppered with shimmering icicles, and snow covered the red roof. Spreading out in both directions near the back of the lodge were two long buildings that made up the main hotel, and farther out were dozens of tiny private cottages, each one a miniature version of the main lodge tucked away into the trees. In the distance, chairlifts worked their way up the mountain and I could see dozens of tiny skiers shooshing down the slopes. A beautiful couple walked by hand in hand wearing matching Patagonia gear, their skis slung over their shoulders. It was a winter wonderland.

"Whoa," I heard myself say.

The driver laughed. "You are going to be just fine."

He pulled up in front of the long covered walkway that led to the front door. A guy about my age in a white coat stepped forward to open the door.

"Welcome to the River Lodge, Miss," he said with a smile, taking my hand to help me out of the car. Damn, he was cute. If every guy who worked at this place looked like that, I could get used to this lifestyle in a hurry.

"Thanks," I replied. Then, even with his help, I managed to trip over the stone-lined curb. An older couple with gray hair and black ski outfits eyed me like I was a drunken hillbilly.

"Oops. There you go," the doorman said, catching me by the elbow.

I fought for composure even though the heat coming off my face could have melted the icicles over my head. "Thanks. First step's a doozy," I joked.

"Happens to a lot of people," he replied.

I smiled at his kindness and was just starting to feel semi-normal again, when I saw a streak of fur rushing toward me.

"Farrah! Sweetie! You're here!"

I held my breath, but not before catching a big gulp of my mother's flowery perfume. As she enfolded me into her mink coat, I caught some of the pelt on my tongue. Gag.

"Let me look at you!"

As she stepped back, I quickly turned and grabbed the animal hair out of my mouth, flinging it from my fingers to the ground. My mother held me at arm's length. Looking into her blue eyes, I was startled by how good it was to see her. I had been dreading her critiques so much I hadn't realized I had actually missed her these last few months. Her dark red hair had grown out a bit so that it grazed her shoulders, and she'd cut bangs, which made her look younger than she already did. As always, her makeup was on the heavy side, but something about her eyes was lighter. Huge diamond studs gleamed in her ears and she was smiling.

"It's good to see you, Mom," I said.

"Don't sound so surprised," she said, smoothing her hair with one hand. "It's good to see you, too. There are literally *hundreds* of Shays and friends-of-the-Shays," she told me, lowering her voice. "They are everywhere. I swear to you, I feel as if I'm invisible."

I smiled at that one. My mother made a point of being larger-than-life. She could never be invisible.

"I'm sure everyone is aware that you're here," I said.

"Well, thank you," she replied. She looked me

up and down and gradually her face fell. I had been expecting this, but my heart still constricted.

"What?" I said tersely.

"Nothing!" she replied. "It's just . . . when was your last haircut, honey?" She reached for one of my curls and pressed it between her thumb and forefinger. "So many split ends."

I rolled my eyes and bit my tongue. Could she be any more predictable?

"Well, not to worry," she said. "They have a four-star salon here. We can have you shaped up in no time."

"Well, thank God for that," I said.

"Are you being sarcastic with me?" my mother asked.

I gave her my best innocent, wide-eyed look. "Of course not."

"Farrah!"

My twin half-brothers, Hunter and Ben, came barreling toward me at full speed and I crouched down to greet them. They both slammed into me at the same time, nearly taking me down.

"Wow! You little monsters sure got strong!" I said, hugging them tightly.

"Farrah! Farrah! Hunter learned how to burp!" Ben announced as I stood up.

Hunter swallowed and burped proudly and I

laughed. Little did he know he'd been burping with the best of them since he was two days old.

"Farrah, please do not encourage them," my mother said as the boys took my hands and started trying to tug my arms out of my sockets.

"Miss? Jeffrey here will bring your bags inside and show you to your private room," the driver told me with a smile as I was jerked back and forth. "It was a pleasure traveling with you."

"Thanks. You, too," I said.

He leaned in toward my ear as he passed me by. "And good luck, Miss."

I grinned in response. He had no idea how much that meant to me. Two weeks sequestered at a mountain lodge with my crazy family and the Shay clan? I was going to need all the luck I could get.

Chapter 2

My room overlooked a skating rink at the center of the hotel complex. It was lovely to gaze down on the gleaming ice, the twinkling lights, and the twirling skaters. A small café stood next to the rink, surrounded by the standing outdoor heaters that were a staple in Colorado. Couples and families reposed under a lattice roof, sipping hot chocolate and watching the skaters. The whole area was draped with thick fir garland, decorated with white twinkle lights and red bows. Wreaths with red berries and acorns adorned every window and door surrounding the rink. It would have all been so peaceful, if Hunter and Ben hadn't been jumping up and down on my bed and screaming while my mother unpacked my bag for me.

"Farrah! Look how high!" Hunter cried.

"I'm higher!" Ben protested.

"Are not!"

"Am too!"

I turned around just in time to catch Ben as Hunter shoved him clear off the bed. If I didn't have the reflexes of a ninja, Ben would have been in for some serious stitches, courtesy of my bedside table.

"All right! Enough jumping," I said, placing Ben on the floor and grabbing Hunter down as well. They responded by chasing each other, screeching, into the bathroom right past Jim—their father—who was standing near the wall watching college football on the TV. I glanced at my mother, waiting for her to discipline the Twin Terrors, but she was busy frowning at my favorite gray sweater, which she held up in front of her like it was a dirty dishrag.

"What were you planning to wear to dinner tonight, Farrah?" she asked.

"That sweater and the pants I have on," I told her.

She clucked her tongue at my black pants and sighed. "We need to go shopping while we're here."

I felt a twinge of hurt and shoved it aside. I was Jane Morris. Jane Morris stood up for herself. Jane Morris knew who she was and liked it.

"No we don't, Mom," I said, taking the sweater from her. I yanked off the red wool one I was wearing and yanked the gray one on over my tank top. "I like my clothes. They're comfortable."

"Well, I have news for you, honey. Being an attractive woman is not about being comfortable all the time," she said as she hung my jeans over a hanger with a grimace.

I stared at her back. Had she just called me unattractive to my face?

"Let the girl be, Liza," Jim said, not taking his eyes off the Michigan game. "She looks fine."

He glanced at me and I smiled in return. Jim didn't say much, but when he did speak he often took my side. I had always been grateful for that, even back in middle school when I resented him for trying to take my father's place. My dad had died of cancer when I was ten, and I had still been devastated by it two years later when my mother and Jim had married. I had given him the cold shoulder for the first four years I had known him, but lately I had finally gotten used to his presence.

"I'm sorry. Is it wrong for a mother to care about her daughter's appearance?" my mother said. "Farrah, I just wish you could be more . . . feminine."

My face stung as if it had just been slapped. I wanted to respond, but my voice was stuck halfway up my throat behind a bubble of indignation. It wasn't as if I hadn't heard it all before. I just wondered when she was going to give it up already.

Just then there was a knock on the door, and Jim, sensing the tension in the room, jumped to answer it. My brother, Jonah, strode in and for the first time I fully understood the phrase "a sight for sore eyes."

"There's my best man!" he announced, crossing the room in two long strides. His hair was cropped short and his face was clean-shaven. He wore a white button-down shirt under a blue sport coat and tan pants, right out of a Shay catalog. Three years ago he never would have been caught dead in an outfit like that, but even as I recognized this, I had to admit he looked incredible. He looked relaxed and happy and tall. I hugged him hard as he lifted me up off the ground.

"Must you call her that?" my mother grumbled.

I grabbed Jonah's wrists as he released me. "Let's get out of here," I said desperately. "Go for an evening ski."

My brother's forehead wrinkled. "You don't ski."

"I live in Colorado now. I had to learn," I told him.

"Well, I'd love to, but we have to go to this dinner in a little while." He checked his watch—a

Rolex, I noticed. Must have been a gift from Marni. That thing could have paid for my tuition. "But we'll definitely do it later in the week. I wanna see what you got."

He knocked me in the arm with the side of his fist and I grinned. God, it was good to see him. All the muscles in my body had already relaxed and he'd only been in the room for thirty seconds.

"Come on. Marni can't wait to see you. The family's waiting down in the restaurant." Jonah was already headed for the bathroom to wrangle the twins.

"Wait. She has to change," my mother said.

Jonah paused and looked me up and down. "Why? She looks gorgeous, as always," he said with a wink.

I grinned at my mother as I swept right past her and out the door. I had never loved my brother more.

"I just can't believe it's almost here. I've been planning this wedding for a year and it's practically all I've done. Well, I mean, besides my job, Daddy, of course. Don't want you to think your little girl is slacking off! But really, it takes up so much of my time and I really just don't know what I'm going to do once it's over! I'm going to need a new hobby!"

I bit my tongue to keep from laughing as Marni babbled, touching her father's arm here, grabbing my brother's hand there. Her straight-as-a-pin blond hair was pulled back in a black velvet headband and she wore a pristine white shirt and huge red beads around her neck—the style of the moment, of course. But unlike the other socialites and fashionistas of our generation, Marni was not about being blasé and über-cool. For fifteen straight minutes she had talked without taking a breath, and the furrows in her father's brow had grown noticeably deeper. Still, each time the waiter approached, Brendan Shay waved him off with a surreptitious lift of his hand, not wanting to interrupt his daughter. Meanwhile, her mother— an elder version of herself—hadn't blinked in a very long time, and my own mother was simply enthralled. Jim had kept himself busy for the duration by consuming half the rolls in the bread basket. My stepfather was never much for talking and I got the feeling he appreciated Marni mostly because, when she was around, he never had to say a word. I was glad the hotel had been holding a kids' party in the game room for the boys to go to. They never would have been able to sit still through all of this.

"But enough about me. Farrah, I have to know."

Marni laid her French-manicured fingers down flat on the table. "What do you think of your dress?"

"I—"

"It's gorgeous, Marni. Absolutely gorgeous," my mother interjected. "You and your mother have exquisite taste."

Mom shot an obsequious look at Mrs. Shay, and Mrs. Shay smiled politely in return. "Thank you, Liza."

Mom beamed. Like a "thank you" from Mrs. Brendan Shay was a commendation from the queen of England.

"I'm so glad you like it," Marni added. "But what do you think, Farrah? I want you to be completely comfortable."

I glanced triumphantly at my mother at Marni's use of the dreaded word "comfortable." Here was the daughter of one of the most respected fashion designers in the world—and the VP in charge of his teen clothing line—telling me she wanted me to be comfy. My mother looked away and took a sip of her wine.

"It's great, really," I said. Even though I had yet to try it on and I couldn't imagine ever being comfortable in a skirt that big. Or any skirt, for that matter.

"I'm just psyched to see this kid in a dress,"

Jonah said, reaching over to knead my shoulder. "I don't think that's happened since her first communion."

"Oh! I bet you looked so cute all in white lace with the veil and everything!" Marni cried, clasping her hands together. "Did you have a veil?"

"She kept tearing it off and ruining her hair, so I finally gave up," my mother said. "But she did wear the tiara," she added, looking at me with a nostalgic gleam in her eye.

"I did wear the tiara," I admitted with a sigh. Though I had laid it in the center of the driveway and crushed it with my bicycle tire later that same day.

Marni's mother quickly checked her watch and exchanged a look with her husband. Mr. Shay glanced at the one empty chair at the table, then looked over his shoulder toward the door of the restaurant. Instantly, the young waiter appeared at his side, taking this as his cue.

"Yes, sir. Would you care to order your appetizers?" he asked hopefully, eyeing our closed menus.

"Actually, we'll be waiting for our whole party to be seated," Mr. Shay replied with an apologetic smile. "But we wouldn't object to another round of drinks."

The waiter bowed and quickly moved away,

clearly relieved to have something to do. We appeared to be his only table for the evening. I guess people like the Shays were given special treatment at hotels like this one. All the other waiters in the place looked pretty darn busy.

"Where *is* Buffy, anyway?" Marni asked, folding her perfectly manicured fingers together. A tiny line appeared just above her nose and looked completely out of place on her otherwise perfect face. "We told her seven for dinner, didn't we?"

"We're so sorry about this," Mrs. Shay said, addressing my mother and Jim. "Our youngest is always late. But we're really looking forward to introducing her to all of you."

"You're gonna *love* her, Farrah," Jonah assured me.

"Oh, completely. You two will *completely* hit it off," Marni asserted with a wide grin.

I eyed them dubiously. What were these two on, anyway? Me and some girl named Buffy? I had my doubts.

"Ah! Finally! Here she is."

Mr. Shay stood up and turned toward the door, and both Jonah and Jim followed suit, like we were living in the 1800s or something. I wondered what other polite mannerisms my brother had picked up from being around the Shays so often.

Lifting myself out of my seat a bit, I strained to see this Buffy chick around the standing men, but they were blocking my view. I really hoped Jonah and Marni didn't expect to saddle me with some preppy poseur the whole time we were here, because if they did, then—

"If you guys ordered me a steak, it better be mooing."

Buffy yanked out the empty chair and dropped into it, tossing her silver-and-black skull bag in the center of the table and knocking over the vase full of rosebuds. Her blond hair was cropped short and spiked and she wore purple eye shadow, black liner, and a silver nose ring. Her ripped T-shirt read DROP KNOWLEDGE, NOT BOMBS and she wore it over a denim mini, cropped black leggings, and red lace-up boots.

I think I was a little bit in love.

Mr. Shay cleared his throat and forced a bright smile as his wife righted the flowers and slipped the offending purse under the table.

"Everyone, this is our youngest, Buffy," Mr. Shay announced as he took his seat. "Buffy, this is Mr. and Mrs. Janssen and Jonah's sister, Farrah Morris."

"Hi, Buffy," I said happily.

She looked at me and sucked at her teeth. "It's

Biff. The only people that get away with calling me Buffy are the sadists who cursed me with the name. Anyone else calls me Buffy and they die."

"Charming," my mother said under her breath.

"That's our Buffy," Mrs. Shay said with a laugh.

Scratch what I said before. I *was* a little bit in love.

Chapter 3

"Can you believe they're getting married?" Biff asked me, lighting a match from a book using only her thumbnail. The flame swelled and sizzled for one moment, then she shook it out and lit another. "I mean, what's the psychotic rush, you know? What is she, knocked up or something?"

"Omigod. She's *not* pregnant, is she?" I said instantly.

"Uh, no. Marni is so repressed I wouldn't be shocked if she was still a virgin."

Biff got bored with the matches and tossed them off my balcony with a flick of her wrist. The resort was all but silent now, many of the lights in the rooms across the way long since extinguished. Biff was staying with her family in one of the ridiculously expensive cottages on the outskirts of the grounds—kind of a long walk in the cold and the dark—but she had shown no intention of making the trek any time soon. I got the feeling she wanted to spend as little time around her family as possible. Which was kind of weird because, even though she was so different from her parents, they seemed to tolerate her—even admire her a bit. Whereas all I'd ever done was not spend money on clothes and makeup, and my mom just couldn't wrap her brain around me at all.

Biff lifted her feet and brought them down on the one empty chair at the glass table, then tilted her head back and groaned dramatically. I hugged my coat closer to myself against a stiff breeze. Suddenly her head popped up again. Her eyes, already big due to all the eye makeup, had grown even wider.

"Wait a minute. You don't think *that's* why they're getting married, do you? So they can do it? Do you think they're, like, *waiting*?"

I snorted a laugh. The very idea of my brother having sex made me want to burn out the area of my brain where my imagination lived.

"I don't even want to think about that," I said.

Biff looked past me for a moment, considering, then shuddered. "Yeah. Good point. So what about you?" she asked, looking me up and down as she recrossed her feet.

I blinked, confused. "What about me, what?"

"You! Ever done it?"

I blushed hard enough to combat the wind and sat back in my chair.

"I'll take that as a no. Got a boyfriend?" she asked.

"No."

She raised one eyebrow. "Girlfriend?"

"No!" I protested. "No. I like guys. Unfortunately, they don't feel the same way about me."

Biff dropped her feet to the ground with a thud and sat forward. "Why not? You're smart. You're hot. What's the deal? Are ya smelly or something?"

I laughed and pushed my thick curls back behind my ears. "Um, I'm not hot."

"Oh, God. Don't tell me you're one of those," Biff said, rolling her eyes.

"One of those what?" I asked.

"One of those pretty girls who pretends like she doesn't know she's pretty," Biff said, lifting her hands up like she just couldn't deal.

"No! Are you kidding? Look at me. I'm *not* pretty." I sat up, frustrated. "I'm pale. I'm freckled. I have this hair that no one can do anything with." I lifted my curls and let them flop down again. "And the worst offense of all, of course, are these," I said, pointing at my non-chest.

"Okay, pale is good when your skin is like cream.

Freckles are cute. Red hair is hot. And it doesn't matter if your chest is small as long as the rest of you is built to match, and you are totally in proportion," Biff rattled off. "You're a babe, Farrah. Admit it."

"Hate to disappoint you, but the only guy who ever even kissed me told me he couldn't date me because I was practically a guy," I snapped. "Is that the kind of thing a person says to a babe? I don't think so."

I couldn't believe I had just said that. That story was one of my deepest, darkest secrets and I'd just used it to defend my stance that I was not hot. The thin mountain air must have been affecting my brain.

Biff gaped at me. "No. That's not the kind of thing a human being says, full stop."

I looked down at my fingernails and picked at them, letting my hair fall forward again. "Well, I beg to differ, because this guy actually said it."

"Was he the devil himself or just one of his minions?" Biff asked.

"Neither," I said with a small laugh. "He was Tommy McNabb and I was totally in love with him. Everyone was totally in love with him, actually. You know those guys that every girl in school has a crush on?"

"I've encountered the subspecies," she said flatly.

"Well, anyway, we ended up kissing in this closet at a party a couple years ago and it was like a dream come true for me." I laughed bitterly at the memory of my total naïveté. "I thought we were going to go out, hold hands in the hall, go to the prom, all that crap. But instead he just shattered me."

"That sucks. What an ass," she said.

"I don't know why I'm telling you this," I replied.

"I hypnotized you. It's just something I do for kicks," she joked. "So please tell me you kneed him in the balls."

"I wish," I said. "I basically fled. All I wanted to do was avoid him for the rest of my life, but of course his parents are good friends with mine, so that was impossible. I'm pretty sure they're flying out for the wedding."

"Is the jackass coming with them?" Biff asked, looking suddenly like she was ready for a fight.

"No. Not invited. Jonah never liked the guy," I said.

She narrowed her eyes and nodded appreciatively. "I knew Jonah was good people."

"I'm not looking forward to seeing the McNabbs, though," I said, slumping. "All they ever talk about when they see me is when are me and Tommy going to get together already."

"Why don't you tell them you already did get together and he dug your heart out with a spoon?" Biff asked.

"Please. They would die."

"So?" Biff said, throwing her arms wide. "Don't you think they should know how rotten the fruit of their loins has become?"

My heart felt sour and heavy, just like it did whenever I thought about that humiliating night with Tommy. I squirmed back in my chair and lifted my knees under my chin. "Can we not talk about this anymore?"

Part of me expected Biff to protest, but instead she shoved her chair back, making an awful scraping noise that echoed off the mountains. In the perfect silence I was surprised it didn't cause an avalanche, but maybe that only happened in movies.

"Fine. Let's get out of here. Let's do something. I'm bored."

"It's one o'clock in the morning."

I wasn't tired, either—thanks to all those all-nighters I'd pulled recently, my inner clock was all out of whack—but what the heck did she expect to do at a posh, conservative resort at one A.M.? This place was no spring break–style destination. Everything closed at ten or eleven.

"So? I'm starving. Are you hungry?"

"Always," I replied. "But I think all the restaurants shut down for the night."

"So?"

"So . . ."

Biff slid open the glass door to my room and shot me a wicked smile that made my skin tingle. "So, let's go eat."

I felt like I should be tiptoeing as we moved through the empty halls on the first floor of the hotel, but I didn't need to. The carpet was so thick it absorbed every footstep soundlessly. Aside from the humming of the ice machine and the occasional ping of a far-off elevator, the place was silent as a tomb. Still, I was pretty sure my heartbeat was audible from about a mile off. I had no idea what Biff was up to, but I knew it was making my nerves sizzle.

"Where are we going?" I whispered as Biff peeked around a corner.

"Stop asking me that," she said.

She moved into the next hallway and boldly walked straight down the center. We were flanked on one side by the entrance to J. P. Steakhouse, the restaurant where we'd had dinner, which was now roped off with one of those velvet swags, and on the other side by the ballroom where the wedding reception would be taking place. There was no one around, but I knew instinctively that we were *not* supposed to be there.

Biff disappeared into an alcove and shoved through a door. It swung closed in my face and I paused. The gold placard in the center of the door read EMPLOYEES ONLY in ornate script. I was about to turn on my heel and retreat when the door opened again and my heart left the building. I half expected to see an angry hotel manager bearing down on me, holding Biff by the scruff of the neck. But Biff was still alone.

"You coming or are you just gonna stand there looking lame?"

The door closed again. Okay. Enough was enough. I slipped through the door and grabbed Biff's wrist. The sounds of water whooshing and a radio playing at high volume made my heart pound even harder.

"This is stupid," I whispered hoarsely. "Let's go find some vending machines. They've gotta have them around here somewhere."

She shot me a look like *Could you* be *a bigger loser?*

"Or what about your cottage thing? It's got a

kitchen, right?" I suggested.

"Oh, yeah. And it's fully stocked with my mom's Kashi cereal and my father's favorite boutique lager. No, thanks," Biff replied. "Now follow me."

Biff edged along the wall until we came to a wide opening. Light poured out from a room to our left, while up ahead everything was dim—almost dark. Biff stood on her toes and strained her neck to see into the well-lit area, then waved her hand at me to follow and jogged forward on her toes. I swallowed my fear and quickly followed. From the corner of my eye I saw at least four guys all dressed in white, chatting and laughing as they hosed off hundreds of white plates. Their backs were to us as we rushed by and one of them turned up the volume on their radio, drowning out their own voices.

By the time I got to the main kitchen area, Biff had already opened one of the huge, stainless-steel refrigerators and had practically climbed inside of it. She shoved aside bottles and Tupperware boxes, opened a few things, sniffed them, and pushed them back inside, all the while making the biggest racket ever.

"Keep it down a little!" I admonished, crossing the huge kitchen quickly.

"Nobody can hear me," Biff said into the fridge. I had to admit, I had barely even heard *that*.

"What are you looking for?" I asked.

"Aha!" she announced. She came out with a big white box and whipped it open on the closest counter. Inside was three-quarters of the seven-layer chocolate cake Biff had ordered for dessert. "This stuff was killer."

She yanked open the closest drawer, jangling the insides at a decibel that made me want to pee in my pants, and fished out two large spoons.

"Spoons?" I said as she handed me one.

"Tastes the same no matter what you eat it with," she told me.

She pulled a stool over, then used it to climb up onto the counter where she sat down next to the cake box and curled her legs up story-style. She dug a huge chunk out of the side of the cake and stuck half of it into her mouth. Her eyes rolled back in ecstasy.

"Mmmmm. You'd better jump in before I scarf this whole thing myself."

"Shouldn't we, like, take it back to my room or something?" I asked.

Biff's arms slumped at her sides. "God, Farrah. Jonah and Marni told me you were cool. But you're, like, the conscience I never had, and it's getting irritating."

My face colored and I glanced away. "Thanks a lot."

Her face fell. "Sorry. Tough love. I'm just trying to get you to live a little."

"I get that," I said. "But this . . ."

Really made me uncomfortable.

"What's gonna happen, really?" Biff asked. "If someone finds us here, which they won't, what are they going to do? Kick us out? Between the wedding and all the rooms he's rented, my father practically owns this place for the next few weeks."

"Okay, okay," I said. "We'll stay."

"Good." She slapped her rings down on the countertop with a clang. "Now get on up here."

Reluctantly I climbed up onto the countertop and sat across from her. Even though my stomach was now in knots, I dug into the cake and took a bite. I felt all the tension instantly melt away.

"Oh my God. This is the best cake I've ever tasted," I said.

"Did I tell you?" she replied.

I took another bite, then got down from the counter and fished a brand-new jug of milk out of the fridge. Searching the place for glasses seemed like a chore, and a loud one at that, so I just took a swig from the jug and brought it back to the counter for us to share.

"I knew you were brilliant," Biff said.

"It just shows, doesn't it?" I joked. After a few more bites and a few sips of milk, I decided to find out more about my new sister-in-law-once-removed. "So, Biff. What's your deal?"

"My deal?"

"Yeah. What do you like? What do you do? Do you go to school?" I asked.

"I go to Bennington in Vermont. It's . . . fine. And I'm the black sheep, obviously," she said, bowing her head slightly.

"I don't see that. Your parents seem to worship you," I replied.

"They do. On some level," she stated. "But they don't get me. Never have. Never will. Marni, they get. Me, it's like the stork brought the wrong baby. I'm not interested in the family biz, I don't want to go to the country club, I have zero interest in the Hamptons."

"Really? I thought everyone wanted to be in the Hamptons," I replied.

"Not me. We have a house in Maine that's much more my speed. Grumpy fisher dudes, cold water, thick forest that could hide any freaky danger you can imagine," she said. "I just sit out on the porch and make up stories about the people

40

there and the stuff I see. That's a vacation."

"So you're a writer?" I asked.

"Sort of. Maybe. I don't know. I just know I'm not a businesswoman like the rest of the fam. Nothing with numbers," she replied. "Numbers suck."

I laughed and licked some chocolate frosting off my finger.

"What do you want to do?" Biff asked me.

"I'm going to be a reporter," I told her. "Hopefully on ESPN."

"ESP what now?" she asked, arching one eyebrow.

"ESPN. You know. The sports network?" I said.

"I don't follow," she replied blankly. "What is this thing 'sports' of which you speak?"

We both cracked up and took another spoonful of cake. I was surprised to see how much the hunk of chocolate had dwindled. We'd eaten almost half of what was there.

"Someone's gonna get in trouble for this," I theorized, guilt seeping into my chocolate buzz.

"But it's not gonna be us," Biff replied, sucking the chocolate off her spoon.

At that moment we heard a door slam from somewhere behind Biff. Her eyes widened in panic and I flew off the countertop, taking the box of cake with me. Biff grabbed the jug of milk and shoved her spoon into her mouth. We wildly scanned the room. There had to be a place to hide in here. Footsteps were rapidly approaching and I could hear someone muttering to himself. Biff grabbed my wrist and dove to the floor, taking me with her. My knee slammed into the tile and I bit my lip to keep from shouting at the pain. We both shimmied behind the butcher's block and I tucked my foot out of view just as the inner door opened.

"Freakin' rich bitch snobs," some guy said under his breath. There was a loud bang as he tossed something down, then a shaft of light appeared as he opened one of the freezers. "Like I have nothing better to do in the middle of the night than run up and down the hill with ice buckets. There's plenty of ice outside. Why don't I just bring you a pick? I can think of a few things you could do with it."

Biff hid a laugh behind her hand and I widened my eyes at her in warning. "*Sorry!*" she mouthed.

I adjusted my weight but misjudged and came down right on my throbbing knee. I winced and my leg automatically shot out and slammed into one of the metal cabinets. The clang reverberated throughout the room, and Biff clenched her hand over mine, cutting into my flesh with her torn fingernails. Our visitor, of course, stopped talking. My heart was in my throat.

"Who's there?" he demanded.

Biff let out a sigh and rolled her eyes. We were screwed and we both knew it.

"All right, whoever you are, I've got a cleaver and I'm not afraid to use it," the guy said.

He tiptoed toward us. There was nothing we could do. We were totally and utterly trapped. Biff and I huddled close together, and I swear I could hear *her* pulse racing. My knee continued to throb, but I barely noticed it through all of the paralyzing fear. I saw his black hiking boots, moist and laced with salt from melted snow, just seconds before his face appeared, hovering over us. My jaw dropped so fast I think it popped. The incredible green eyes staring down at us widened.

"Jane?"

Looking down at me was Hot Connor.

Chapter 4

"Jane?" Biff repeated, confused.

I shot her a silencing look that I could only hope she would understand, and unfolded myself from the floor. Connor reached out and took my arm and hoisted me up. My already pounding heart went spastic. Hot Connor had just touched me. Was still touching me, actually. His hand was clasped around my forearm as he stared at me in unadulterated shock.

"Wh . . . what are you doing here?" I stammered.

"I work here," he said. That much was obvious. Not only was he in the kitchen in the middle of the night, but he was wearing a full suit and tie under his puffy River Lodge down parka, and his normally sexy-stubble-covered face was perfectly clean-shaven. And still gorgeous, of course. "What are *you* doing here?"

Behind me, Biff stood up, kicking the cake box

back under the butcher's block and out of sight.

"Oh, we were just . . . we got lost. I mean, this place is huge and I took a . . . a wrong turn and I—"

Connor laughed. It was a nice laugh. "No, I don't mean here in the kitchen. Even though I am curious. I mean here at the lodge."

"Oh." Duh, Farrah. "I'm here for a wedding."

Instantly something in his face shifted. It was like his eyes clouded over. He released his grip on my arm and I felt a sudden chill. Whether it was from the sudden lack of contact or the complete change of attitude, I wasn't sure. I suppose it was both.

"You're kidding," he said. "You're with them?"

Biff and I exchanged a look. That had not been a good tone.

"Them who?" Biff asked.

Connor looked at both of us and I could practically see his brain working, realizing he'd already said too much. "Nothing. Forget it," he said, waving a hand and turning away. "You guys really shouldn't be back here. You should probably—"

"No, really. What were you going to say?" Biff prodded, leaning into one of the countertops. "Because if you're talking about all the overprivileged snobs running around this place like they own it, we're not *with* them."

"You're not?" Connor asked doubtfully.

Biff looked at me and pursed her lips, trying to get me to back her up. Unfortunately I was still so stunned by Connor's presence, my brain was having trouble catching up, and I had absolutely no idea where she was trying to go with this.

"Uh, no. No. We're not," I put in, feeling lame.

"But if you're here for the wedding . . ."

"Yeah, we're nannies," Biff said. "For the Janssen family? The groom has these two little brothers. We take care of them."

"Seriously?" Connor asked. He was clearly pleased by this news. He looked to me for confirmation. "You're a nanny."

"Girl's gotta make a living somehow," I improvised.

"Wow. That's so cool. So then you know. I mean, what they're like," Connor said, opening one of the freezers. He grabbed an ice bucket and started filling it up using one of those plastic shovels. "It happens every time they book a wedding here. You've got to be a billionaire to afford this place, so whenever we have one the hotel is overrun by these spoiled snobs who have no sense of boundaries. They think they own the lodge and everything here is theirs. Bunch of morons with names like Misty and Hoyt descend on us and take over, doing whatever they want and blaming whatever they steal or break on the staff."

Biff snorted a laugh at the names he threw out, savoring the irony of the moment, of course. Little did Connor know he was talking to two people named Farrah and Buffy. Meanwhile all I could think about was how very solidly he'd pegged us. We'd already devoured pretty much an entire cake as if it was ours, and most likely one of those dishwasher guys would get blamed for it. I felt ill all over again.

"It drives me out of my mind," he said. "Like tonight, for example. This will be the third run I've made to one of the outer cottages to bring ice to this woman. Why? Because she didn't like the cubes in the first two buckets. No. Her ice has to be round."

Biff looked at me and cringed. *"My mom!"* she mouthed. I had to slap my hand over my mouth to keep from laughing.

Connor turned around and slammed the freezer door. He placed the bucket down on the counter and took a deep breath, then smiled at us.

"Sorry. I'm not usually this clenched. I just had to get that off my chest. I should be used to this by now. I've been working here since I was fifteen and there's at least one of these big society parties every Christmas. I guess I should be happy that this year there's only one," he added, his eyes apologetic.

God, they were beautiful eyes. I stared into them, mute, for a long moment before I suddenly realized I was expected to talk. I cleared my throat.

"No problem," I told him. "This is Biff, by the way."

Connor offered his hand to Biff and they shook. "Nice to meet you."

"Charmed, I'm sure," she teased.

Connor smirked. "So . . . what were you guys doing in here, anyway?" he asked finally. "Because no one's buying that 'we got lost' line."

I bit my lip and shot Biff a helpless look, then turned and retrieved the cake box, spoons, and milk jug from underneath the butcher's block. "We had the munchies. Sorry."

Connor looked at the mangled cake and laughed. "No problem. They were probably just gonna chuck that anyway. They don't serve day-old cake at the River Lodge."

"God forbid," Biff said.

"Exactly," he replied. "It's good someone got to enjoy it."

"Oh. We did," I assured him.

Connor smiled, sending a pleasant shiver all

through my body and curling my toes. I seriously could not believe that after wishing all semester for the guts to talk to him, I had done just that twice in one day. And now it looked as if we were going to be in semi-close quarters for our entire break. How had I gotten so lucky?

"Hey. How'd that last final go?" he asked.

A thrill shot through me. Had he just been thinking about our last encounter, too?

"Fine, I think." *Even though I was fantasizing about you the entire time I was taking it.* "How's your leg?"

"It's healing nicely," he said. "Thanks for asking."

"You, too."

We stood there for another moment, grinning at each other, until Biff finally kicked the underside of the metal counter. The resounding clang woke me up.

"Sorry," I said to Biff.

"What? No. That was just a twitch," she replied innocently.

"I'd better get back to the ice queen anyway," Conner said, lifting the bucket. "Don't want her complaining to my boss."

"Which she totally would," Biff said under her breath.

"Yeah. She seems like the type," Connor

replied. "I'll see you guys around."

"Definitely," I replied.

He shot me one last smile before lifting his hood over his head and ducking through the door. I quickly gathered up the cake and milk to put them back in the fridge, using the massive door to hide my extreme giddiness until I could regroup. When I closed the door again, composed, Biff was right in my face.

"So, *Jane*," she said. "Care to explain?"

"Oh! My! God! You guys!" Marni shrieked, her face turning dark pink as she lifted yet another piece of black lingerie out of a box. She held it up for everyone to see, and all her friends clapped and whistled. As far as I could tell, this one was all straps and nothing else.

"What do you do with that?" I whispered to Biff as Marni held the garment, as it were, up against her white sweater and laughed.

"It looks like a slingshot to me," Biff replied.

"That one's from me," Calista McBride announced. She swung her dark hair over her shoulder and took a sip of her mimosa. "I heard Madonna bought one the day before I was in the shop so I just *had* to get it for you."

"I think that's the tenth name she's dropped,"

Biff whispered to me. "I should be keeping score."

I smiled and stared at Calista's profile. I still couldn't believe I was in the same room with Miss Paparazzi Magnet herself. When I was in middle school, Calista McBride had starred for two years in one of those crappy teen TV dramas and everyone had followed every move she made. Since then she had become a staple of the New York party scene and was constantly getting caught drinking in places she shouldn't be or hooking up with other starlets' boyfriends. I hadn't even known that she and Marni were friends until I'd walked into the room and saw them posing together for an *InStyle* photographer.

"I don't get it. She and Marni seem like polar opposites," I said.

"They are, but they've known each other since kindergarten. Marni swears that Calista is a good person deep down," Biff said, placing her hands over her heart jokingly. "Personally, I think she's black as tar deep down."

One of the other guests, a petite, wispy girl with shoulder-length brown hair, leaned over to inspect the garment. "Omigod, Calista. It's divine," she gushed. "You have the most incredible taste."

I turned my head and whispered to Biff, "Does that girl just agree with everything Calista says and does, or is it just me?"

"Carina? Yeah. She's a never-thought-for-herself type, and she worships Calista," Biff whispered back. "See how their outfits are almost exactly the same, just different colors?"

I glanced at the ladies and noted that their clothes were, in fact, very similar, down to the shape of the heels on their pumps.

"Weird," I said.

"Yeah. They've been like that since they were kids," Biff told me. "I'm pretty sure 'Carina' is actually Carina's middle name, but she uses it because it's similar to Calista. Frightening."

I stared at Carina as she tossed her hair back, just as Calista had done a moment ago. For a split second I actually felt sick to my stomach. The girl seemed nice enough and was pretty in her own right. If she was close with Marni, that meant she'd gone to all the right schools and had every advantage, and yet she couldn't even form her own personality? How sad.

"Oh, come on! Is there nothing but lingerie here?" Marni cried, lifting a long, red, see-through nightgown out of another box.

"Well, it's not like we could give this stuff to you at your *real* shower," one of the women protested. "There were congresswomen there!"

Marni laughed, and I looked out one of the huge windows that overlooked the ski slope. This bridesmaids' brunch was being held in the Club House at the very top of the mountain, and the view was absolutely breathtaking. Much more interesting than the pile of slut gear Marni's friends had apparently amassed for her. Stuff she was supposed to wear for my brother. The very idea made me want to gag. I wished Marni hadn't insisted I attend, but in her opinion I wasn't just a best man but an honorary bridesmaid. At least the food had been stellar. Blueberry pancakes with bacon and fruit salad. Although I was pretty sure Biff and I were the only ones who'd actually eaten the pancakes.

"Don't look so gloomy," Biff told me. "At least you didn't have to go to the real shower. That was all oohing and ahing over pots and baking pans and spoonulas."

"Spoonulas? What the heck is a spoonula?" I asked her.

Biff shrugged. "Some kind of torture device for when the man gets out of line, I assume."

Marni's next gift was a tiny Yankees tank top and a pair of pinstriped boy shorts. Now that was some lingerie I could get behind.

"Oh, Jenna! Is this from you?" Marni said. "How cute."

"I figured I had to get it," Jenna Regino, daughter of a New York State senator, told her. "Remember that night we went to the sports bar with Jonah with all the—"

"Omigod! The peanut shells!" Marni cried.

I looked at the two of them and felt this hot stab of jealousy. They had gotten to watch the World Series with Jonah while I had been alone in my dorm in my Yankees cap, calling him between innings.

"Yes! And he was like, 'Strike him out! Strike him out,'" Jenna chanted, laughing. "I thought he was possessed or something. I mean, God. Like they haven't been in the Super Bowl before."

"It's the World Series," I blurted before I could stop myself.

Twelve perfect heads of hair swung around and suddenly all eyes were on me. Calista, who had appeared on newsstands recently doing the walk of shame in nothing but a minirobe and duck boots, by the way, looked me up and down like I was some kind of mountain troll who'd just rolled in the door.

"What?" Calista demanded.

"In baseball it's the World Series," I said, feeling a conspicuous heat crawling up my neck and into my face. "The Super Bowl is football."

Calista sneered at me, her eyes falling on my still-wet-at-the-hems jeans. "Well. I suppose *you* would know."

"Um, as someone who's bedded the entire New York Jets offensive line, shouldn't *you* know?" Biff asked.

Calista's eyes flashed and for a brief moment I thought we were going to have a catfight on our hands, but then she became all angelic sweetness. "Oh, Buffy. You're *so* witty. Have I ever told you how much I appreciate your wit?"

"Gee, Calista. Thanks ever so much," Buffy replied in an equally saccharine tone.

"All I meant was, Jonah and his sister are obviously very close, so clearly she would know all about sports because Jonah knows all about sports," Calista explained.

Biff and I looked at each other. We both knew that wasn't what Calista had meant. She'd meant that since I was the only one in the room wearing jeans, hiking boots, and no product, obviously I would know all about sports. Even Biff was semi-dressed up, sporting a funky plaid skirt and chunky black sweater. Honestly, I could not figure out how they all managed to look so coiffed. We'd all had to take the chairlifts up the mountain to get here. How had they done it in stilettos and silk? How had they kept their hair so perfect? It was fascinating to me.

"Jonah and Farrah *are* really close," Marni said, jumping in to diffuse the tension. "Did I tell you guys Farrah is going to be the best man?"

Calista snorted. "Good. So you'll be able to wear pants to the wedding as well."

A few of the other girls laughed lightly. My mouth opened, but no sound came out.

"Actually, I got Farrah a gorgeous Monique Lhuillier," Marni said, her voice firm. "I think she's going to put the rest of us to shame."

That seemed to bring an end to the idea that Marni was going to let any of them get away with insulting me. I could have kissed her for coming to my rescue. I didn't much care what these girls thought of me, but I did feel a huge sense of relief when they finally tore their assessing eyes off my clothes and returned their attention to the bride. I smiled my thanks to Marni and she nodded quickly in return.

"So. Who's next?" she asked, looking around for another gift.

The door to the Club House opened and my heart caught in my chest. Connor stood not three feet away, holding the door for two catering staff members who were carrying in the cake. At first I hoped he would just duck right out again, but instead he closed the door and went to help with the dessert setup.

"Oh, crap," I said under my breath.

"Just try to look natural," Biff whispered back.

As Connor crossed the room I saw him do a double take from the corner of my eye. *Snagged!* I looked over and lifted my chin to acknowledge him. Biff raised her hand in a wave. Connor looked extremely confused, but to his credit, he didn't interrupt the proceedings. He simply went about his business and shot us one more bemused smile on his way out.

"How are we going to explain that the Janssens' nannies were at the bridal shower?" I asked Biff.

"I'll think of something," she replied. "I always think of something."

"Well, that's it! Thank goodness!" Marni said, standing up. She took a sip of water and straightened her wool skirt. "I'm feeling a little warm after all that!"

Her friends laughed and the circle of chairs they had formed to watch Marni open her gifts broke up. A few of them went over to admire the cake and get themselves some more fruit salad, while Marni walked over to me and Biff. We stood up as well and I stretched my arms over my head. I'd had a late night, and the encounter with Connor, plus the massive amounts of chocolate I'd consumed right before bed, hadn't helped me fall asleep.

"How are you guys doing?" she asked, touching my arm. "I'm sorry. I had no idea they were going to give me all that stuff."

"It's okay," I said. "I'll just have to forget everything I've seen here today."

Marni laughed and tossed back her hair. "I'm sure it's not half as bad as what the guys will do for Jonah at his bachelor party," she said. "How are the plans coming along?"

I stared at Marni. "Plans? For what?"

"For the bachelor party," Marni said. "When are you having it?'

I felt as if the entire mountain had just crumbled beneath me and suddenly I was looking around for something, anything, to grab on to. I was supposed to plan a bachelor party? No one had told me that! How could I not be informed about this? And what the hell did *I* know about bachelor parties?

Marni gradually started to recognize the panic that must have been written all over my face. Then she started to panic as well. She grabbed my arm and squeezed.

"You did plan a bachelor party, right? Farrah! You're the best man."

"I . . . it's—"

"Of course she planned a bachelor party!" Biff said, shoving her sister's shoulder. Her voice took on this larger-than-life quality, not unlike Marni's. I guess she knew how to speak to her sister in her own language when necessary. "She just doesn't want to talk to *you* about it! You're the bride!"

Relief flooded Marni's eyes and she laughed, holding a hand to her chest. "Oh, thank goodness. You had me scared there for a second. Jonah would freak out if he didn't get to have a bachelor party. It's all he's talked about for weeks."

All he's talked about? Well, he could have talked to *me* about it!

"Well, he will *not* be disappointed," Biff said, still speaking Marni-style. "Right, Farrah?"

What would I have done without her? "Definitely," I replied. "It's gonna be great."

Fictitious, but great.

After the brunch was finally over, I found out exactly how Marni, Calista, and the other girls had arrived at the top of the mountain looking like beauty queens on parade. They had actually taken a shuttle bus—a half-hour drive up a winding road—while I had thought the chairlift was the only option. Of course, had I known, I probably would have taken the chairlift anyway. It was peaceful up there, hanging above the slopes. The view was breathtaking and it took about a third of the time, so that was exactly how I was going to get back down as well. Together the other girls all loaded into the van with Marni and her gifts while Biff and I stood at the door of the Club House and waved.

"Okay, how the hell am I going to throw a bachelor party in the next ten days?" I demanded the second the last door had closed.

"It's gonna be fine," Biff said, walking back inside. "There have to be strippers in Colorado somewhere."

She went right over to the pay phone by the bathrooms and yanked out the phone book.

"Strippers?" I croaked, leaning back against the wall. "I have to get my brother strippers?"

"It *is* a bachelor party," Biff said. She flipped through the flimsy pages quickly, snapping each one. "Do you think they'd be under exotic dancers?"

"It's just, I don't know if Jonah is a stripper kind of guy," I said, weary at the very thought of all the decisions that lay ahead of me. Not to mention the idea of watching my brother and a bunch of his friends shove dollars into some topless chick's G-string.

Biff leveled me with a stare. "*All* guys are stripper kind of guys."

Just then a door at the end of the hallway opened and out walked Connor. He was wearing a light blue shirt and khakis today and had a small gold plate on his pocket with his name stamped into it. It was amazing how he was just as hot as a responsible concierge guy as he was as brooding, disheveled college boy.

"Good morning, ladies," he said with a smile.

"Hey," I replied, pushing myself away from the wall.

"Whaddup?" Biff said, still flipping pages. God, I really hoped she didn't ask Connor for stripper recommendations. A girl could only take so many embarrassments in one morning.

"So, you guys were at Marni Shay's bridesmaid's brunch?" he asked, his brow knitting.

"Oh, yeah . . ."

I looked at Biff. Wasn't she supposed to come up with some kind of explanation for this? Didn't she "always"? But Biff simply ducked her head closer to the book and kept flipping. Apparently she had yet to come up with a story. Gulp.

"Yeah, well, we . . . we're really close with the family," I stammered. "My . . . Mrs. Janssen—my boss—she says we're practically like daughters. So she gave us the morning off, and Marni was nice enough to invite us."

Whoa. Had I just said all that? And more important, had Connor bought any of it?

"Well, that's nice," he said with a quick, thoughtful frown. "Maybe this particular wedding party isn't so bad after all."

I smiled. "Yeah. They're pretty cool. Most of them anyway," I amended, picturing Calista's snotty face.

"Cool. Well, listen, I'm glad I bumped into you again, actually," Connor said, crossing his arms over his chest. "A bunch of people are going to hang out tomorrow night and I wanted to see if you guys wanted to come. If you can get away from the kids, I mean."

Biff dropped the phone book now, suddenly alert. "Hang out? You mean, like a party?" she asked.

"Yeah, kind of," Connor told her. "The staff does it at least once a week to blow off steam. So, you girls in?"

"Totally," Biff replied.

"What about work?" Connor asked.

"Oh, they go to bed early and then we're pretty much free," I told him quickly. "We should be fine."

"You don't have to ask your boss first or anything?" he asked dubiously.

I glanced at Biff. It was so past time for her to help me out here.

"Oh, we will, but I'm sure it'll be fine," she said, waving her hand.

"Cool. I'll swing by your room around nine?" he suggested.

"Sounds like a plan," I told him.

Connor grinned. "Okay, then. I'd better get back to work. I'll see you tomorrow."

"Yeah. See you tomorrow."

Connor walked down the hall and paused outside the Club House kitchen to talk to another member of the staff. I couldn't believe it. I had a date with Hot Connor! Well, a group date, but still. It was a social thing and he had invited me. Us. Whatever. I had to call Dana, like, now.

"He knows something's up," Biff said, looking after Connor.

"What do you mean?" I asked.

"He's clearly not stupid, *Jane*," she said. "If he doesn't see us with your brothers soon, he's going to start asking questions."

"Good point," I replied. "I guess we're gonna have to spend some time with the Twin Terrors."

Biff's eyebrows shot up. "The Twin Terrors? Wow, sounds like fun."

"Oh, but it'll be worth it," I said, watching Connor as he checked something out on a clipboard. The sun pouring through the windows made his hair shine like gold. "It'll definitely be worth it."

Chapter 5

I stood at the bottom of the hill as Hunter came careening toward me on his big yellow tube. His face was pink from the cold and his blond hair stuck out from the front of his black knit cap. I checked my watch and then stuffed my hands back into my pockets. The sun had long since disappeared behind a thick layer of gray clouds and the wind was starting to kick up. My skin had tightened to my face like plastic wrap about half an hour before and my nose was starting to run. Luckily the hour of snowtubing we had paid for was almost up. I was very much looking forward to getting the boys inside for some hot chocolate. All I could hope was that the last hour of nonstop activity had tired them out a little bit. No wonder my mother had been so utterly grateful when I'd offered to babysit. These kids gave off more energy than a nuclear power plant.

"Whoo! Go, Hunter!" I cheered, clapping my

mittened hands. They stung like mad every time they smacked together.

Hunter laughed and rolled off the still-moving tube a few yards before it slid right into my feet. Then he jumped up and came running over to me, as fast as his snow pants and big boots would let him.

🍂 "Farrah! Farrah! Did you see me? I went fast!" he shouted happily.

"Yeah! You so did!" I said, crouching down to his height. "Look! Here comes Ben!"

I turned Hunter around and put my ice-cold cheek next to his as Ben whooshed down the mountain. His tube turned around so that his back was to us and for a second I panicked, thinking he might get scared if he couldn't see where he was going. But when he turned around again, he was laughing like a crazy person. He stayed in his tube all the way down to the flat part of the hill and slid right by us, cracking up the whole way.

"Uh-oh. Where's your brother going?" I said lightly to Hunter.

Hunter shrugged, though you could hardly tell, what with all the clothing he had on. We turned together and jogged to catch up with Ben, who had finally come to a stop right outside the snack bar.

"Nice run, Benny!" I said, lifting him out of his tube.

"Let's go again! Again!" Ben cried.

"Oh, I'm sorry, kiddo, but that was your last run," I told him. "Our hour's already up. But maybe we can go inside and—"

"No! I wanna go again, too!" Hunter shouted.

"Yeah! No fair!" Ben cried. "Let's go again!"

"Maybe we can come back another day," I pleaded. "There has to be something else you guys want to do."

"I wanna snowtube! I wanna snowtube! I wanna snowtube!"

I closed my eyes and prayed for patience. Or for some act of God to save me. It was almost Christmas, wasn't it? Where was my Christmas miracle?

I heard footsteps crunching along the packed snow and opened my eyes again. A pair of black hiking boots stepped into view. "Having some trouble?"

Connor. Of course. He would have to see me *now* when the boys were having one of their tantrums rather than sometime in the last hour or so when we were having all kinds of fun together. I pushed myself up, and Ben immediately grabbed the strap on the tube from my hand. He started trying to drag it and Hunter back toward the rope tow and was getting nowhere fast. Seemed like it would keep him occupied for a while, so I just let him keep trying.

"They're just tired," I told Connor, who was bundled into a big black parka with fur around the hood. "Problem is, they don't know it."

Connor grinned and instantly my skin warmed. Maybe if he stuck around I could actually tolerate the cold a little longer. He was like my very own space heater.

"Well, where's Biff? Shouldn't she be helping you?" he asked.

Biff had been forced to go shopping for hair accessories with her mother and Marni. Apparently the ones they had ordered for the bridal party had not turned out the way Marni wanted so they had to find some new ones, stat. Of course, I couldn't tell Connor that.

"Yeah, well, she's . . . she's kind of got a cold," I improvised. "I didn't think she should be out here in this weather."

Ben gave the tube a good yank and ended up on his butt.

"Well, I'm off work now if you want some company," Connor offered. "Kids love me."

"Oh, do they?" I asked teasingly.

He grinned. "I'm very lovable in general, in case you hadn't noticed."

Oh, I had.

"You really don't have to do that," I told him.

Connor shrugged and pulled a pair of big snow gloves out of his pockets. He tugged them on like a doctor going into surgery. "I want to. Besides, I've got some time to kill."

While I was pretty much dying to jump at the chance to spend the rest of the day with Hot Connor, my logical side was making a few decent arguments. First, if he hung out with us, he would be tortured by the Twin Terrors and might never speak to me again. And second, my brothers were sure to call me "Farrah" any second now, and then the whole jig would be up. So, of course, being first and foremost a woman of logic, I said, "Okay. Sure. We'd love to hang out with you. Right, guys?"

Ben and Hunter were now working together to push the tube toward the rope tow. They both stopped, however, and looked up at Connor like they had just realized he was there.

"Who's he?" Ben asked.

"Is he your *boyfriend*?" Hunter sang.

"No! He is not my—where did you even learn that word?" I sputtered.

But Connor laughed. "Just let me go clock out," he said. "I'll be back in a minute."

"Okay," I said happily.

The second that Connor was gone, I dropped to my knees in the snow again and pulled both Ben and Hunter to me by their hands. This time they didn't resist.

"All right, you guys, for the rest of the day we're going to play a little game," I told them. "No matter what happens, I want you guys to call me Jane, from this moment on. Understand?"

"Why?" Ben asked.

"Because that's the game," I told him.

Ben pondered this, then asked, "How do you win the game?"

"You win if you don't say the word 'Farrah' once for the rest of the day," I said, trying to be patient and feeling like at any second Connor was going to walk right up behind me.

"What do you win if you win the game?" Ben asked.

Good lord! What was this, *Hardball*?

"You win . . . um . . . " I looked around, as if a trophy and prize package were going to fall right out of the sky.

"How about we get to keep snowtubing?" Hunter suggested, narrowing his eyes.

I rolled mine. This kid was way too smart for his age. "Yes. Fine. One more half hour. But then that's it."

"Yeah!" Hunter cheered, pumping his fist.

"Okay, but if you're Jane, then I wanna be Spider-Man!" Ben said, jumping up on his toes.

"Oh, yeah! And I wanna be Wolverine!" Hunter put in.

I laughed and took the strap on the tube. "Fine. I'm Jane. You're Spider-Man and you're Wolverine."

"What's your *boyfriend's* name?" Hunter teased.

Hot Connor? I thought. "Just Connor," I said. "And he's not my boyfriend."

"Farrah and Connor sittin' in a tree!"

"It's Jane!" I wailed.

"Oh. Yeah. *Jane* and Connor sittin' in a tree!"

I shook my head and dragged the tube toward the rope tow. This was going to be an interesting afternoon.

"Okay, what are you doing, exactly?" I asked Connor.

On his knees in front of me, he packed a wad of snow into a perfectly formed snowball and added it to a pyramid of other perfectly formed snowballs. Together with the boys, they had already made about a hundred of the things, and I must admit I was a tad wary of what was going to happen next.

"Don't worry about it," he told me, flipping his blond hair off his face to look up at me with a smile.

Sigh. Whatever you say, Sir Gorgeous. Sheesh. Maybe I *shouldn't* date this guy, even if by some miracle it turned out he wanted to date me. I mean, if he could get me to forget basically everything that was going on with one small smile, that could be dangerous, right?

"If you say so," I replied, leaning back on my hands.

I was sitting in a shaft of sunlight on a log bench near the pine grove at the back of the resort's property. The clouds had passed, leaving behind that bright blue Colorado sky I knew and loved, and allowing the sun to warm up the afternoon just enough to keep me from calling it quits and retreating inside. After another hour of snow-tubing, the boys had still been raring to go, so Connor had suggested coming back here to play a game of Duck and Weave. Whatever that meant. I had yet to find out, since all we had done since arriving among these majestic, towering trees was make snowballs.

"Okay! I think that looks like enough," Connor announced finally, pushing himself up off the snow-covered ground. "What do you guys think?"

"Yeah!" the boys cheered. Even though they had no idea what the snowballs were for, either. Those two were always excited to just move on to the next event.

Connor slapped his gloved hands together and rubbed them, looking down at the boys. "Right. Now here's how we play."

He reached for my hand, and my heart skipped so many beats I thought I might need a defibrillator. Still, somehow, I managed to put my mitten into his thick glove and he pulled me up from my seat. We stood together in front of the boys.

"Jane and I are going to run and hide and you guys are going to take these snowballs and try to pelt us with them," Connor announced.

"We are?" Hunter said, practically salivating.

"They are?" I asked, wondering how I had gotten suckered into such a thing.

"Yes. You are," he addressed the boys.

"Do we get to pelt them back?" I asked.

"Uh, no," Connor replied, his brow creasing. "That's why it's called Duck and Weave instead of . . . Pelt and Pelt."

All righty then. I had been wondering all along what Connor's faults might be. Now I knew. He was obviously totally bonkers. This thought must have been clearly reflected in my eyes, because

Connor leaned toward me and said, "Just trust me, okay?"

Once again, the lowered, husky voice sent shivers right through me.

"Okay," I replied.

I was hopeless.

"All right. We're gonna go hide. You guys count to ten, then come after us," Connor instructed the boys. "Ready?"

The boys nodded, all determination and excitement. Hunter eyed the snowballs hungrily.

"Go!"

Connor grabbed my hand again and pulled me toward the trees. I was so taken off guard, my feet went out from under me and I almost took a header right into the snow. Luckily, however, I was able to right myself before diving into utter humiliation. Behind us, Hunter and Ben counted at the tops of their lungs.

"One! Two! Three!"

"Come on! Come on!" Connor laughed giddily.

"I'm trying!" I replied, slipping on the snow. I really needed new snow boots. These things clearly had no traction.

We ducked through the tree line and went a few more feet before Connor pulled me behind the thick trunk of a pine, holding my back to him with his arms around my waist. My breath was already short from the run, but now I felt almost dizzy.

"What're you doing?" I said before I could rethink it.

"Hiding," he replied, directly into my ear.

I thought I was going to melt right then and there. It took my brain a long moment to de-fuzz, but when it did, I realized I had to act cool here. Like the hottest boys on campus were pulling me behind trees and hugging me to them every day of the week.

"Um . . . what's with this game? We don't even get to defend ourselves?"

"Ten!" the boys shouted. "Here we come!"

"First of all, they're six years old," he said. "How hard can they throw?"

"You'd be surprised," I replied, listening to their little footsteps drawing closer. "Their father has been drilling them in quarterbacking and pitching since before they could walk. I think he's already requested applications from all the PAC-10 schools."

Connor blinked. Clearly he didn't know my family. Well, the family for which I nannied.

"Well, regardless, the whole point is to tire them out," he said.

"I hate to be the one to break this to you, but

they're devil spawn. Devil spawn don't tire out," I joked.

"They will. Think about it. How many snow-balls can they carry at a time? Three? Four tops," Connor whispered quickly. "They throw them at us, then they gotta run all the way back there for more, then chase us down again. Then run back for more. These kids'll be in bed before dinner."

I tilted my head back to look at him. His mouth was *right there*. I tore my eyes away from it and looked into his eyes instead.

"I like the way you think," I told him.

"Thank you," he replied, gazing down at me. Was it just me, or had his eyes just trailed down to my lips?

"Got you!"

Smack! I was hit directly in the face by a snow-ball. My cheek exploded in pain, and cold snow dripped down my cheekbone and into the collar of my turtleneck sweater. Have I mentioned that Hunter is going to be a major-league pitcher when he grows up?

"Oh! Ow! Are you okay?" Connor asked, wincing as he inspected my face. Honestly, when I saw the concern and apology in his eyes, I stopped feeling a thing. Then another snowball hit the tree just to the left of his head.

"Forget about me!" I cried, laughing. "Save yourself!"

"Right. Go! Go! Go!" Connor cried, shoving me away from him.

We split up, running in opposite directions, as I used my mitten to wipe the cold and wet off my face. Ben came after me while Hunter ran after Connor. I ducked behind another tree, and Ben launched three snowballs straight into the bark.

"Reload!" he shouted.

Then he turned and ran back toward the pile of snowballs. Meanwhile, a few yards away, Connor let Hunter hit him in the back with a snowball and did a big, dramatic near-death scene, arms flailing, legs staggering.

"He got me! *Augh!* He got me!" Connor lamented, crawling toward me.

I laughed as Hunter celebrated behind him.

"But I'm not dead yet!" Connor shouted, jumping up again. "Better go get some more ammo."

Hunter dropped his arms and narrowed his eyes like he'd been played, but then turned and ran for more snowballs.

"Nice one," I said, slapping hands with Connor.

"Ready for round two?" he asked, his green eyes dancing.

Behind his head, I saw two pom-pom-topped heads bouncing toward us. "Let's go!"

And this time I grabbed his hand and pulled him with me deeper into the woods. Always better to have someone in the foxhole with you in the middle of a heated battle. Especially if that someone was Hot Connor.

Chapter 6

"*Glad you're feeling better*, Biff," Connor said as he led us along a well-trodden path through the trees, the beam of his flashlight bouncing along rocks and snowdrifts. "When Jane told me you had a cold, I figured you wouldn't be able to make it tonight."

"Oh, yeah. Well, I'm DayQuiled to within an inch of my life," Biff responded, shooting me an irritated look. I had forgotten to tell her she was supposed to be under the weather. Of course, she hadn't missed a beat anyway. "In fact, there's a good chance I'll be talking gibberish by the end of the night."

"I look forward to that," Connor teased.

"*Sorry*," I mouthed to Biff. She shrugged it off.

"So, where're we going?" Biff asked, looking up at the tops of the trees, which effectively blocked out the darkened sky above. "Don't take this the wrong way, but I haven't known you that long and if you're taking us up here to ax-murder us, I'm going to be really pissed."

"Biff!" I said, whacking her arm with the back of my hand.

Connor laughed. "I'm not going to ax-murder you," he said. "Can't speak for my friends, though."

Just then we heard a whoop from somewhere nearby, followed by a burst of laughter. Moments later we stepped into a large clearing centered by a roaring fire in a rock fire pit. Drawn up around the fire were stadium chairs and coolers of various sizes, while at least a dozen people milled and mingled. Flashlights and lanterns of various shapes and sizes hung from the lower branches of several trees to light the small clearing. It looked like the crowd was made up mostly of guys, but I spotted at least two girls, both golden-haired, huddled together and whispering to each other on one of the coolers.

"Davy! There you are!"

A burly guy wearing not nearly enough clothing stepped toward us, a beer bottle raised in greeting. He had a thick beard, even though he couldn't have been more than twenty, and wore a torn Iowa State sweatshirt over a thermal. His hat was one of those leather aviator things with fur earflaps and it was pulled low over his forehead.

"How's it going, Paulie?" Connor said, slapping hands with the guy.

"Better now. I mean, look what you brought," he added, looking Biff and me up and down. "Nice."

"Um, ew," Biff said, crossing her arms over her chest.

"You know you love me," he replied.

"Get me one of those and we can talk about it," Biff replied, nodding at his beer.

Paulie, who was already nicknamed Paul Bunyan in my mind, dropped his jaw slightly. "Really?"

Biff rolled her eyes and took his arm, yanking him toward the nearest cooler. The guy tripped forward, stunned, but was soon grinning and fishing a beer from the ice.

"Wow. Your friend works pretty fast," Connor said.

"Well, so does yours," I replied, though I had a feeling the only reason Biff had gone off with Paul Bunyan was to give Connor and me some privacy. For a girl I'd only known a few days, she was really going all out to help me, bless her twisted self.

"Want something to drink?" Connor asked me, lifting his hand in greeting to a couple of guys across the way.

"I'm okay for now," I said.

"Then let's . . . grab that rock," he suggested.

We walked over to a low rock close to the fire, and Connor unfolded a flannel blanket he had tucked under his arm. He spread it across the rock, then held out an arm, inviting me to sit first. Such a gentleman. I perched on the rock and held my hands out toward the fire as Connor slapped hands and chatted with one of the guys. I could feel the two blond girls looking at me, and my face started to heat up under their scrutiny. I pushed my curls behind my shoulder and tried to look like I hadn't noticed them. Soon, however, they had stood up and were strolling my way.

Okay, just be cool, I told myself. *If these girls are friends with Connor, I'm sure they're perfectly nice.*

"Hey, there," one of them said. "I'm Laura and this is Gin."

"Gin?" I asked.

The girl tilted her head and her hair fell perfectly over her shoulder like a shampoo ad. "Short for Gina. I hate Gina," she said, scrunching her nose.

"I can relate," I said. I felt awkward, tilting my head back so far to talk to them, so I pushed myself up. That one small change in altitude morphed me into the abominable snowwoman. I had about six inches and twenty pounds of muscle on both of them.

"Bad name?" Gina asked.

"Yeah. It's . . ."

Oh crap. I couldn't tell them my real, hated name.

"Jane," I finished lamely.

"That is bad," Gin said, sipping her wine cooler. "Talk about blah."

"Yeah. Blah," I said, relieved and insulted at the same time.

"So, Jane, you're staying at the hotel?" Laura asked.

"Yep," I replied.

"And you came here with Connor," Gin said, studying me.

"Yep," I replied again.

"It's amazing, isn't it? How the guests always go after Connor?" Laura said to Gin as if I wasn't even there. "I mean, what do they think he's gonna do, hook up for a week?"

"Yeah. If they took the time to know him at all they'd know he's not that kind of guy," Gin added flatly, looking me in the eye.

Well. This conversation had just taken a nasty turn. I was so shocked that I couldn't think of a thing to say, which meant that I was just standing there looking guilty as charged.

"These East Coast girls always think they can just snap their fingers and have whatever they want," Laura put in. She flicked me a disgusted look and glanced away to swig at her bottle.

Okay, Farrah. Time to defend yourself. Time to channel your inner Jane.

"I—"

"Actually, Jane may be an East Coast girl, but she's not one of *them*. She's working here, just like you guys," Connor said, stepping up next to me. I lifted my chin and felt the angry, embarrassed heat start to dissipate from my face. "And also, I know her from school, so if we were hooking up, it would be for longer than a week, believe me."

Laura and Gina both gaped at that proclamation, while I absorbed the full implication of what he'd just said. Had he just mentioned hooking up with me? Had he just implied that he *wanted* to hook up with me? I pressed my lips together to keep from laughing out of sheer nervous giddiness.

"At least, I'd hope it would be," Connor said, looking down at me.

I smiled, my heart pounding like crazy as I gazed back up at him. There were no words in my head, but I found that I didn't need them. Just staring at each other like that was enough to make both Laura and Gina slink away. Connor reached out and tucked his hand into the pocket of my coat, pulling me to him. My breath caught in my throat as our thick jackets pressed together. Connor smiled and started to lean forward. My pulse pounded in every inch of my body. He was going to kiss me. Hot Connor was going to kiss me!

Smack!

Connor was hit in the side of the neck with a snowball, which exploded and pelted me with a dozen tiny shards of ice.

"Why does that keep happening to me?!" I blurted, wiping the icy water from my face.

Connor turned and we both saw Paul Bunyan laughing and pointing at us. Actually he was more cackling than laughing, while Biff rolled her eyes and shook her head next to him.

"You are *so* dead!" Connor shouted, dropping to the ground for some snow.

Suddenly everyone was shrieking and ducking for cover. Snowballs flew from all directions, taking out empty beer bottles, sizzling into the fire, and occasionally landing on their mark. I raced over to Biff, clutched her hand, and ducked behind a large boulder.

"I'm so, *so* sorry!" she gasped. "I couldn't stop him!"

"It's okay. It's not your fault," I told her as snowballs whizzed overhead. "But he was going to kiss me, right? I wasn't imagining it?" My heart was still beating a crazy, erratic beat that was both exhilarating and almost uncomfortable.

"Lip lockage was inevitable," she replied. "All you've gotta do is get him alone again and he's yours. So much for that theory that you're not hot."

I couldn't believe it. Seriously. Of all the girls at school and all the girls at the resort, how could he possibly pick me?

"Looks like Nanny Jane has snagged herself a boyfriend," Biff teased, nudging me with her elbow.

And suddenly I felt my giddy high melt away slightly. Nanny Jane. Connor hadn't picked me, Farrah Morris. He'd picked Nanny Jane. What on earth had I gotten myself into?

Ten minutes later, the snowball fight still raged, thanks to a group of guys who had joined the party late and immediately launched an assault on the rest of us. Biff and I tried to mount an offensive from behind our rock, but we were clearly out of our league. These people were born and bred in the snow. And did they ever know how to fling a ball.

"I can't take much more of this," I said, squeezing my eyes closed as ice balls exploded all around me.

"Think we can make a crawl for it?" Biff asked, nodding toward the trees.

Out of nowhere, Connor came launching over the rock and crouched down next to us. His face was all red and blotchy and dotted with pellets of melting ice. His green eyes were bright and alert, like a man ready for action.

"Come on. I'm getting you out of here. This is no place for a lady," he joked.

"Wow. Someone has a serious hero fantasy," I teased.

"Hey, if you wanna stay, then fine." He started to stand up and took a snowball right in the shoulder. I grabbed his hand and yanked him back down.

"You know a way out?" I asked.

"Are you kidding? I practically grew up out here."

I glanced at Biff. "Go!" she mouthed, looking at Connor's back meaningfully. "Go with him!" Then she closed her eyes and pantomimed making out, wagging her tongue and moving her head around.

I laughed and shook my head, but she stopped the second Connor looked at her.

"What about Biff?" I said, trying to cover.

"I'll be fine! Save yourselves!" Biff cried dramatically. She grabbed a snowball and stood up, flinging at random, then crouched down again. "Just go! I'll cover you."

"Thanks, Biff," I said. "I owe you one."

"You owe me many," she replied.

"On the count of three," Connor said, taking my hand. He looked at Biff. "One, two, three!"

We ran out of there, crouched close to the ground, as Biff launched her snowballs into the fray. A few stray bits of ammo flew in our direction and someone shouted after us about how chicken we were, but we just kept running. A few minutes later we were free and clear. I laughed as we walked down the hill.

"That was fun," I said. "Kind of *Saving Private Ryan*, but fun."

"It could go on for an hour," he said. "Those guys don't know when to quit."

"Well, then I'm glad we bailed. I'm not much of a soldier."

"And this way we actually get to talk," Connor said with a smile.

My heart warmed. Maybe this whole thing

was intended to be an actual date. Pinch me now.

"So how do you think you did on Granger's final?" Connor asked as our feet crunched through the snow.

"Oh no! No school talk," I said, lifting a finger.

"Come on! You know you want to go over it. A grade-obsessive like you doesn't not want to figure out how she did," Connor told me.

"How do you know I'm a grade-obsessive?" I asked indignantly.

"Possibly because you're always the first person out of your seat at the end of class when she's returning papers," he said with a laugh. "You go through those things like a coyote goes through garbage."

"There's a nice visual," I said, snagged. "So now I'm a rabid dog?"

"Coyotes are not dogs. And no one said anything about rabid," he shot back. "Besides, I happen to think coyotes are beautiful creatures."

I blushed and stared down at my feet as they crunched through the snow. He was right, of course. I did look forward to every grade with a sort of dreaded excitement. But all I really cared about at that moment was that he had noticed it. The more I talked to Connor, the more clear it became that he had been watching me almost as long as Dana and I had been watching him. Hard to believe, but apparently true. Maybe Biff was right. Maybe I *was* hot.

"So? Tell me. Which essay question did you pick?" Connor asked me as we approached the first of the outer cottages. "You picked the one comparing and contrasting the Brontë novels, didn't you?"

"Uh, no," I told him. "Please. Give me a little credit."

"No way. You tackled the Dreiser question?" He whistled. "You're even braver than I thought."

I beamed at the compliment and decided right then and there that I was getting that kiss by the end of the night. No more of this self-doubt, no more guilt over the fact that he thought my name was Jane and I was a nanny. I mean, my name *was* Jane—I'd decided that at the beginning of the year. And I was helping my mom take care of the kids. I hadn't misled him that much. And I wanted to kiss him, dammit. I really, really wanted to kiss him.

I had just made my kiss resolution when something moved in the woods. I jumped, startled, and a tree branch snapped. Connor steadied me and stared into the trees.

"So much for that bravery," I joked.

"*Shhh,*" he said, his eyes darting around.

Suddenly I felt like I was going to faint. "What?

Is it a bear?" Oh, God. I was going to die. Mauled by a bear before I ever even got to smooch Connor.

"No. It's them!" Connor cried. "Run!"

At that moment, Paul and a bunch of the other guys rushed out of the darkness, launching a sneak snowball attack. Connor grabbed my hand and sprinted into the trees on the other side of the path.

"Die! Die! Die!" someone shouted. I screamed as a snowball hit my back and droplets of freezing water slithered down my neck.

"This way!" Connor said.

He was tearing through the woods like a wolf, dodging trees and stumps and rocks like they were nothing. I did my best to keep up and was actually quite proud of myself. I only tripped once and slammed into only one tree. Our attackers fell behind quickly and before I knew it, we had emerged onto one of the paved pathways near the outer cottages of the resort.

"Omigod!" I said, my heart pounding. "What is wrong with those people?"

"They're insane," Connor replied, breathing hard. "Come on! I know the perfect hiding spot."

We raced down a short pathway toward what looked like a dead end, but then he turned again and I found that we were inside a hidden back entryway to the hotel, the door camouflaged by a rock wall and a few large pines. Connor pulled me into the corner and locked his arm around me, drawing me in so that we were as small as we could possibly be. I felt his warm breath on my face, but all I could hear was the pounding of my heart and his friends' running footsteps.

"Come out, come out, wherever you are!" a voice sang nearby.

I almost laughed. I couldn't help it. But Connor put his hand over my mouth and shook his head, his eyes dancing. Whoever this guy was, he was right on the other side of the wall. If either of us made a noise, we were toast.

"Come on, you guys! I bet they went back up the hill!" someone else shouted. Then the footsteps turned away from us and gradually faded to nothing. I started to relax and pull away, but Connor held me firm, and my heart caught.

"Do you think it's safe?" I asked.

"I don't know. I think we should maybe stay here a while longer," he said, his words breathy. "Don't you think?" he added with a grin.

I stared at his lips. "Yeah. Seems like a good idea."

And then, *finally*, his lips touched mine. His kiss was warm and soft and strong and firm all at the same time. It was completely and utterly perfect. It melted away any leftover guilt and replaced it with a fullness I'd never felt before. Connor wanted me. He really, really wanted me. And as of that moment, I was his.

I couldn't sleep. I just kept replaying that kiss over and over and over again, staring at the ceiling and laughing to myself. If there had been a hidden camera in the room, whoever was watching the feed would have thought I was a mental patient. Sometimes, my recollections were more vivid than others, and at those moments I had to cover my face with a pillow and scream.

Connor had kissed me. Hot Connor had kissed me. He really liked me. Would we be going back to school a couple? Connor Davy and Jane Morris. It had kind of a ring to it.

Okay. I was getting ahead of myself. *Dial it down a bit, Farrah.* But I didn't want to. This was too much fun. I could allow myself a daydream or two, couldn't I?

I rolled over onto my side, clutching my pillow beneath my cheek, and imagined what an actual date with Connor might be like. In my fantasy, there was a knock at my door. I lifted myself ever so slowly out of my chair, wearing my black best man's dress. My hair was twisted up into an elegant 'do with little tendrils down around my face. In my mind I had actual cleavage and wore just the slightest bit of makeup. I carried myself like Marni Shay would—all straight-backed and untwitchy. I was, basically, my own polar opposite.

When I opened the door, there was Connor, wearing a killer black tuxedo and looking oh-so movie star. When he saw me, his breath was taken away. I imagined that part about ten times. It had never happened to me and I longed to know what it felt like. To have a guy look at me and be stunned by my beauty. I would never admit that longing to anyone, but alone in my room I could admit it to myself. I wanted Connor to look at me like I was a supermodel. Like I was the only girl in the world.

Without a word, Connor reached out and pulled me to him. My heart stopped right there in the bed, just imagining it. Suddenly it was all around me. The scent of his skin, the feeling of his light stubble against my cheek, the softness of his lips . . . his tongue. In my mind he kissed me again. And again and again and again, until I finally drifted happily off to sleep.

Chapter 7

Jonah and I were out on the slopes first thing the next morning. He'd been skiing a lot longer than I had, because his best friend from high school, David Gelb, had a house in Vermont and used to take Jonah up there every other weekend in the winter. But even though he could have taken on the black diamond runs, he stuck with me on the yellow and was beyond impressed at my skill. Actually I was rather impressed myself. I was doing better than I had any of the other four times I'd gone with my friends, and I had a feeling I had my adrenaline high from the night before to thank. I felt more energized and more relaxed, and everything seemed crisper and brighter and sweeter. All thanks to Connor.

After warming up with a few easy runs, Jonah and I decided to race down one of the trails. We trash-talked each other all the way—"Eat my powder," "You couldn't handle a bunny slope in

Jersey," that kind of thing—earning some disturbed looks from parents and some appreciative laughs from other kids my age. When I beat him to the bottom, I couldn't stop laughing. If only the whole week could be like this. Me and Jonah hanging out, me giddy over having just been kissed. It all combined to make me forget about everything else.

"I can't believe I'm getting married next week," Jonah said as we waited for the chairlift to scoop us back up the mountain.

I swallowed a lump of dread that formed in my throat and sat, pulling the bar down. "Are you excited?"

"Yeah, definitely. And scared out of my mind," he admitted with a laugh.

"You think maybe you shouldn't do it?" I blurted.

Jonah's eyes sparkled. "No. Of course not. Nothing like that. It's just a big step. You know, like when you left for college, you were scared, right? But you knew you wanted to do it."

I leaned back and gazed up the mountain. "I was too psyched to get the hell out of Jersey to be scared."

"Right. I forgot. You hate our hometown and everything in it," Jonah teased, nudging me with his elbow.

"Well, not everything," I told him, nudging him back.

Jonah smiled and looped his arm over my shoulder. I rested my head against him and sighed. I loved my brother so much, sometimes it hurt. Before my father had gotten sick, we were just like any other brother and sister that were born four years apart. I irritated him and he tortured me. But once we started to really understand what was happening to my father, everything changed between us. My mother was always at the hospital, so we were dropped at various friends' and neighbors' houses all the time to eat unfamiliar food and live by unfamiliar rules and sleep in unfamiliar beds. All we had during that time was each other, and it formed this bond that was unlike anything I'd ever had with anyone else. Ever since then, Jonah had been my protector, my advisor, and my best friend. Sitting with him there, knowing how drastically everything was about to change, I felt a fullness in my heart.

"I just want you to be happy, you know," I said, my voice cracking.

"I know," Jonah said, giving me a squeeze. "I'm sorry I've been MIA so much lately. Everything will calm down after the wedding."

It's almost embarrassing how relieved I was by those simple words.

"So, fill me in. What's been going on with you lately?" Jonah asked, pulling away to look at me. "How were finals? Any guys I have to interview and intimidate?"

I grinned automatically. I couldn't help it. Jonah's jaw dropped and he leaned back.

"There *is* a guy!" he exclaimed.

I was pretty much dying to tell someone about Connor. I'd called Dana a couple of times, but we'd been playing phone tag.

"Well, yeah," I said. "His name's Connor. He was in my English Lit class."

"What's his deal? Where's he from?" he asked. "Is he worthy? No. Scratch that. No one's worthy."

I laughed. "You think way too highly of me."

"Not possible," he said.

"Well, he's from Colorado," I said, blushing. "And he's so smart. Like he always just had the most insightful things to say in class and stuff. Plus he's really athletic. He rides a dirt bike around campus and he's into skiing and snowboarding and, you know, drinks smoothies instead of coffee."

"So he's a tool," Jonah joked.

"Jonah!"

"I'm just kidding. He sounds perfect for you,

Farrah," he said. He studied me for a moment and I blushed even harder under his scrutiny. "I've never seen you like this," he commented.

"Like what?" I asked.

"Like all giggly and happy and stuff," he said. "I like it."

I smiled and looked up at the ski patrol cabin near the top of the chairlift. My heart felt warm and tingly as I thought about Connor's smile, the way he'd looked at me just before he'd kissed me. "I like it, too."

We slid off the chair lift and grabbed our poles. "So, ready for another run?" I asked, reaching for my goggles.

"Actually I'm starved," Jonah said. He glanced at the larger building next to the Club House where we'd had Marni's brunch. People were skiing in and out and smoke poured from the stone chimney. "Wanna head over to the café? I heard they have some serious muffins up here."

My stomach grumbled at the thought. "I'm in."

We skied over to the entrance and the automatic door slid open. Just inside was a cozy area with benches for skiers to remove their gear before heading inside. Already I could smell the fresh roast coffee and the scent of baking bread. As we sat down to take off our skis, my stomach grumbled even louder. Loud enough for Jonah to hear.

"Why don't I go get in line before your stomach comes out and eats you whole?" he joked.

"Sounds like a plan," I replied.

Jonah headed inside and I slipped my feet out of my ski boots to flex them and roll my ankles. The door slid open again and I glanced up as a family of four skied through. That was when I saw him. Connor. Standing outside the Club House a few yards away. At first my heart caught and I smiled, hoping he would see me, that we would talk, that maybe I'd get another kiss. Then I noticed he was talking to someone. A very beautiful someone.

I didn't recognize the girl, but she was clearly a guest. She wore an expensive white-and-pink ski outfit that hugged every inch of her petite, curvy body. Her dark hair was sleek and perfect and pushed back from her face by a white fleece headband. Her cheeks were rosy, her lips shimmered with gloss, and her eyes were so big and gorgeous I could admire them from yards away. She said something to Connor and he laughed, never taking his eyes off her face. She tossed her hair. He blushed. She touched his arm. He didn't move away. They were flirting. Right there. Right in front of me. And Connor was clearly enjoying himself.

Suddenly I felt as if I was going to throw up. Every inch of my skin prickled with sweat under my thermals. I had to get out of there before I could see more. I stood up quickly and turned around and was instantly accosted by my own reflection in a mirror on the wall. When I saw what I looked like I wanted to die. My skin was chapped and dry and makeup-free. My eyes were rimmed with red from the cold. My hair beneath my cap was wild and stuck out in all directions. My blue ski jacket was shapeless and plain.

My mother was right. I was unfeminine. I was barely even a girl. If any sane man saw me standing next to that ski bunny out there, the choice would be obvious. Sure, maybe Connor liked me right now, but sooner or later he would see me among other actual females and he wouldn't be able to ignore the difference.

"I can't date you, Farrah. You're practically a guy."

Tears prickled behind my eyes. I took a deep breath and turned away from my reflection. I knew what I had to do. And I knew someone who would be more than happy to help me do it.

I found my mother in the hotel's state-of-the-art salon and spa. It took me fifteen minutes to talk my way past the soft-spoken but very determined man at the front desk. He insisted that it was spa policy that no client should be interrupted during his or her treatment, lest it disturb their sense of peace and well-being. Little did he know that what I was about to tell my mother would bring her more joy than she had experienced in the entire eighteen years I had been her daughter.

Finally I told him that this was a female type of emergency. He blanched and let me right through. A woman in a white uniform led me to a small room where my mother was kicked back in what looked like a dentist's chair, her face slathered with purple goo and her entire body mummified in white towels. Her eyes were covered by a blue mask that looked like a flotation device but was filled with some kind of gel. Soft guitar music plinked in the background, and a tabletop waterfall in the corner made me instantly have to pee. Yeah. That was a relaxing feeling.

"Ms. Janssen?" the woman said softly. "Your daughter is here to see you."

"Very funny, Martha," my mother said.

"Mom. I'm really here," I stated in a full voice.

My mother sat up straight and, with no use of her arms, her gel mask plopped down into her lap, then slid to the floor. If I hadn't been so stressed out, the sight of my wide-eyed, purple-faced "mummy" would have probably cracked me up. As it was, I couldn't even smile. Not in the face of the crow I was about to eat.

"Is everything all right? Is it the boys? What have they done?"

Okay. I guess I had effectively shattered her sense of peace and well-being.

"Everything's fine. I just need to talk to you," I said, determined.

My mother nodded to Martha, who slipped out and closed the door behind her. I looked around and found a stool, which I pulled over to my mother's side and straddled. I sat up straight, took a deep breath, then let my back relax.

"Okay, Mom. When I tell you what I'm about to tell you, I need you to promise me that you will not scream, that you will not get too excited, that you will not do anything to make me wish I had never come in here."

"Farrah. You're scaring me here," my mother said.

I closed my eyes impatiently. "Just promise."

She let out a sigh. "I don't know why there has to be so much drama, but fine. I promise."

"Okay." I took another breath and held it. After eighteen years of rabidly opposing every shopping spree, every makeover attempt, every surprise trip to the makeup counter at Nordstrom, I could not believe I was doing this. It took all the strength in my body to get out the next few words. "Mom, I want you to take me shopping. I want a . . . a makeover."

She sucked in air so fast it made a squealing sound in the back of her throat. Her eyes were like pools of sheer delight. I knew that if her hands were free, she would have clapped, then grabbed me and hugged me.

"Mom! You promised!" I snapped, standing up.

Instantly she composed herself, but I could still see a gleeful smile trying to take over her face. There was a sour feeling in my stomach, and I had to remind myself that this was my idea. That I had come to her. That it was all for Connor.

Think of the cute, pink-and-white snow bunny with her perfect hair and her perfect face. She's your motivation, I thought.

"I'm sorry. You're right," she said. "Can I just say one thing?"

I swallowed hard. "Fine. One thing."

"Oh, Farrah," she said, her eyes wet. "I'm just so happy."

Shoot me now. Seriously.

"Now, press that button on the wall," she said, lifting her chin.

"Why?" I asked warily.

"We need to get Martha back in here," she said. "The first thing we're going to do is take care of that dry skin of yours. It ages you at least five years, but a good, moisturizing mud pack should do the trick."

I took a deep breath, let the insult roll off me, and did as I was told. I was doing this for Connor. I just had to remember that. It was time to try being a girl.

The boutique was small and bright and claustrophobic. Maybe they thought that if they cranked up the heat, people would be tempted to take off their clothes and try on some new ones. They were half right. Since walking in forty-five minutes earlier I had shed my heavy coat and my sweater and now stood in between two racks of clothing in nothing but a T-shirt and jeans with the rest of my clothes bunched up over my arm.

"What about this?" my mother asked, holding up a rather skimpy blue dress. I liked the color, but couldn't imagine showing that much skin.

"Nah."

"This?" It was pink and there was an appliqué flower on it.

"Uh, no."

"The flower comes off," she said.

"Still no."

My mother sighed and shoved the clothes back onto the rack. Behind me, I could feel the middle-aged proprietor shooting me disapproving looks. I was starting to think this had been the worst idea of my life. Except for the fact that my skin felt incredible after my spa treatment. It felt soft and light and not at all like my skin. Plus it smelled like lilac. I loved the scent of lilac.

"Farrah, I am at a loss to understand why you asked for my help if you didn't intend to take any of my advice," my mother said, hands on hips.

Even I had to admit she had a point.

"At least try something on," she said, pulling out another garment. "This?"

It was an emerald-green, boat-necked, stretchy top. Almost a T-shirt but fancier. I frowned, considering it.

"That color would look gorgeous with your hair," the proprietor lady offered.

"Fine. I'll try it," I said, snatching the hanger from my mother's fingers.

"I'll find you a skirt!" my mom said happily.

Yeah. Because that was going to happen. I walked over to the dressing rooms and slid into an empty cubicle. Across the way, a girl a bit older than me was changing with her curtain halfway open. She wore a matching set of black lace lingerie, the bottoms like little shorts and the top pushing her boobs up practically to her neck. Feeling my ears redden, I snatched my own curtain closed and stripped down to my plain, white cotton bra. Irritated, I yanked on the green shirt and turned toward the mirror, expecting to take one look at myself and rip it right off. Instead, I paused.

I paused and adjusted it, smoothing out the wrinkles and straightening the sleeves. The color did look incredible with my hair, and it brought out the green flecks in my eyes. Plus, the neckline made me look like I had, well, a neck. And the way the fabric clung to my body . . . I blushed and looked away. Did I actually have breasts?

I glanced back. Yep. I sure did. They were small, but they were there. Right there for all the world to see. I was *so* not used to that. What if guys noticed them? What if people, like, ogled me or something? Actually, maybe this wasn't the best idea.

"Farrah? Farrah, honey."

I peeked around the curtain and saw my mother holding a black skirt shaped like an A.

"Do you have it on?" she asked excitedly.

I nodded, not trusting myself to speak in my

half-giddy, half-embarrassed state.

"Well, let me see!"

I held my breath and opened the curtain. My mother's eyes actually welled. She covered her mouth.

"Oh, honey. You have such a cute figure!" she cried.

The girl in the black lingerie snorted a laugh.

"Mom!" I scolded.

"Sorry! Sorry," she said. "Here. I brought you a skirt."

There was no way I was letting her buy me a skirt, but I took it from her anyway, just so the mortification would end. I let my jeans drop to the floor and stepped into it. The fabric felt silky and tickly against my bare legs as I pulled it up. I did the zipper and button and stared at my reflection.

Let's just say I walked out of there with the skirt, a pair of opaque tights, black ballet flats, the boat-necked top in three different colors, and a fitted, white V-neck sweater. That's right. I shopped. And I actually enjoyed it.

Just call me Farrah Morris, girly girl.

That night, after a huge dinner with the family, I unbuttoned my jeans under my sweater and headed back to my room to watch *SportsCenter*. I couldn't wait to get into my pajama-sweats and sack out on my queen-size bed. One thing about this wedding that was definitely a plus—having my own room with cable for two whole weeks. Back at the dorm we got zero reception on Dana's rabbit-eared TV. The upperclassmen dorms had been renovated and made cable ready, but us lowly frosh had to deal with dial-up connections for our Internet and the torture of watching Rachael Ray in black and white with occasional fuzz. The clear picture on my hotel room TV was like a drug.

I stepped out of the elevator and found Connor standing right in front of me. My hands went right to my waistband, which was sticking into the underside of my sweater and causing an obvious protrusion.

"Hey. I was just looking for you," Connor said.

He was wearing a suit and tie again. Luscious.

"You were?" Behind me, the elevator pinged and the doors slid closed. The hallway was empty. *Kiss me, kiss me, kiss me!* I thought.

"Yeah, I had a break and I wanted to talk to you," he said, scratching behind his ear with one finger.

"Oh? What's up?" *Kiss me!*

"I . . . uh . . . wanted to see if you wanted to do something. With me. Tomorrow night. If you're free," he said.

Was he nervous? Was Hot Connor nervous? And, wait a second. Had he just asked me out?

"Sure. Yeah. Definitely," I said.

Connor's entire face lit up. Like I'd just told him he'd gotten a 4.0 this semester. Or that the whole wedding was vacating the premises tomorrow. That's how excited he was by the fact that I'd said yes. How cool was that?

"Great. I'll pick you up at your room at eight?" he suggested.

"Sounds perfect," I replied. Thank God I had gone shopping with my mother. When he picked me up I was going to look *so* date-worthy. I was going to completely blow him away.

Hopefully.

Chapter 8

The night before Christmas Eve, a light snow started to fall, blanketing the entire resort with a fresh coat of shimmering white. I stood at the window of my room, trying not to obsess about my reflection but instead to focus on the beauty of the scene beyond. On the ice below, a bunch of little kids attempted to make a chain and skate around the perimeter like one long snake, while a woman in white twirled in the center, channeling Sasha Cohen. A full orchestra version of the *Nutcracker Suite* played over the speakers at an unobtrusive volume. It was all so—

Wait a minute. Did I have lipstick on my teeth?

I bared my fangs in the window but couldn't tell if I was just seeing things, so I ran for the bathroom mirror. Nope. No lipstick. Just a figment of my imagination. For the millionth time I smoothed the front of my green top and checked out my skirt from all angles. My hair was back on the sides and I wore lipstick, mascara, and even a touch of eyeliner—under my eyes only. Trying to apply it on my lids had resulted in lots of sweat and tears and, eventually, a second shower and a white flag. I had tried out foundation and powder, too, but that had just made me look like I was trying to hide my freckles and was failing miserably, so I washed it all off. No blush needed, either. My cheeks were plenty rosy with anticipation.

I checked my watch. Connor should be here any second. The thought made my heart pound painfully and I placed my hand over my chest.

Calm down, Farrah, I told myself. *It's just a date. Just . . . your very first date ever with the most gorgeous guy you've ever known.*

Ow. That could not be good. If my heart kept doing that I was going to end up in the hospital by the end of the night.

There was a knock at the door. I whirled around so fast I slammed the back of my hand into the doorjamb.

"Ow!" I cried, shaking my hand out. That was going to leave a mark.

"Jane? Are you okay?" Connor called.

Crap. I hadn't realized I had shouted that loud. "I'm fine!" I called back.

I raced across the room, my heart basically

pounding an escape route through my chest cavity, and grabbed the doorknob. I yanked it open and *slam*! The safety lock was on. I caught a glimpse of Connor's startled face before I closed it again.

I was going to cry. Seriously. Between the pain in my hand, the heart failure, and the embarrassment, I really wanted to cry.

Keep it together, Morris, I told myself. I closed my eyes, took a deep breath through my nose, and rendered myself reasonably calm. Then I unlatched the safety lock, opened the door, and somehow managed a smile.

"Hi. Sorry about that," I said.

"No problem. Happens all the time," Connor replied. "People always put those things on and then forget about them."

He looked me up and down and my pulse fluttered, waiting for his reaction. I looked pretty. I knew I did. I *had* to. I had tried so hard. . . .

But as I stood there, waiting, his handsome face fell. My knees started to quiver. So much for taking his breath away. That particular daydream was right out the window.

"What are you wearing?" he said with a laugh.

A laugh. Oh God. Kill me now. Please, please, please.

"I . . . It's a skirt," I said dumbly, looking down at my legs.

"I know it's a skirt. It's a nice skirt," he said, his eyes smiling. "It's just . . . you can't wear that where we're going."

"Oh." My chest filled up with rocks and mud and sludge. "What should I wear?"

"Just throw on some jeans and a sweater," he said. "It's gonna be cold. I can wait out here."

"Jeans and a sweater." Basically the outfit I wore every single day of my life. "Right. I'll be out in a sec."

I closed the door and stood there for a long moment, struggling to catch my breath. He hadn't even said I looked pretty. Nice. Good. Anything. All he'd done was . . . laugh. My eyes filled with hot tears as I gazed down at my new clothes. I felt like an idiot. Why had I bothered? All that effort for nothing. I didn't know who to be angry at— him, for not seeing me as the type of girl who got dressed up for dates, or me, for trying to be that girl.

I grabbed my most comfortable jeans and a wool sweater and headed into my bathroom to wash my face. Dream Date Farrah was done for the night.

* * *

The wind blew my hair back from my face as we hurtled through the trees. We caught some air and I screamed and laughed with delight, clutching Connor's jacket with an iron grip. We hit the ground again and I slammed into him from behind.

"You all right?" he shouted over his shoulder. I could barely make out his words over the roar of the snowmobile and the whooshing of the wind.

"Are you kidding?" I replied, resting my cheek briefly on the back of his shoulder. "This is awesome!"

What could be better than being forced to cling to him for an hour of heart-pounding, daredevil racing through the snow? I had never been on a snowmobile before, but within the first five minutes of our run, I had decided to save up for one. This was the coolest thing I had ever done, spraying up snow on every turn, shooshing along the trail through the trees. At times I truly felt like we were flying, although I wasn't sure if that was the snowmobile or the rush of being so close to Connor.

Forget the girly outfit. This date was so much better than any fancy dinner.

Suddenly I noticed that the trees were starting to thin and we were making our way up a bit of an incline. The trail was getting slimmer, too, as if not as many snowmobilers had ventured along this route.

"Where're we going?" I yelled. My heart swooped as we hit a patch of ice and the snowmobile skidded sideways. Connor righted it easily, however, and we were back on track in a matter of seconds.

"You'll see! We're almost there!" he shouted back.

Sure enough, seconds later we shot into a clearing. Connor slowed the snowmobile to a stop and glanced over his shoulder at me. "This is it."

"This is what?" I asked. All I could see were trees and rocks and swirling snow.

Connor rolled his eyes in a teasing way. "Trust me. Get up."

I swung my leg over the snowmobile and stood. My legs were unsteady at first. I didn't realize how tightly I'd been squeezing the seat with my thighs. But I managed to stand straight. The last thing I wanted was for Connor to think I was out of shape. He stood up from the mobile and took off his goggles, then reached for my hand. I smiled and slipped my glove into his.

"This way," he said.

Together we followed a trail of footprints through the snow, winding upward on the hill. It was a bit of a hike, and we didn't talk much as we made it. I concentrated on keeping my breathing under control in the thin air, just like I did on a long run. Finally we came to a stop and I looked up at Connor quizzically. He smiled, took my shoulders in his hands, and turned me around.

I was looking down at River Lodge. I could see the entire resort spread out below me, its lights twinkling through the falling snow. Smoke billowed up from the chimneys of the outer cottages and I could just make out the skating rink outside my window. Off to our right, the ski lifts hummed away, carrying nighttime skiers toward the sky. Somewhere, the engine of another snowmobile hummed, and far, far in the distance, cars whooshed along the highway.

"Wow. It's so beautiful," I said.

"It's my favorite view," Connor said. Then he squeezed my hand. "I wanted to show it to you."

"Thanks," I said, turning to look at him.

He stared back at me, his eyes all serious. All I could think about was my red nose and my frizzed-out hair and my sweaty underarms. Snowmobiling was hard work. I remembered how beautiful I'd felt back in my room, all clean and silky. I wished I could feel that way right then.

"I bet you bring all the girls up here," I said to

break the tension.

His brow creased. "Why do you say that?"

My heart panged. That was not a good tone. "Sorry. I was just kidding." God, I sucked at this. He'd been about to kiss me and instead I'd gotten him angry.

"I've never brought anyone up here," Connor said. "I just thought you might like it."

"I do," I said desperately. "Honestly. Forget I said anything. I'm glad you brought me."

Connor took a deep breath and let it out, looking at the view. Away from me. I felt as if the whole night was deteriorating before my eyes. Any second now he was going to tell me I could walk myself back down the hill. I wanted to say something to fix the situation, but I had a feeling I would just put my foot in my mouth again and make things worse.

"I don't date tons of guests," Connor said finally. "Laura and Gin were just being Laura and Gin. They like to pretend they own all the guys that work at the resort just because we've all known one another so long. They were just trying to intimidate you."

"Oh. Okay," I said.

"Maybe some guys take advantage of the situation. You know, a resort always full of women who come and go, but that's not me."

"Oh, I know," I said automatically. Even as a picture of the pink-and-white snow-bunny girl flitted through my mind.

"You do?" he replied.

"Well, I don't know. How could I know? But I figured . . . I don't know," I said. "I'm sorry I said anything."

Connor studied me for a long moment and I could practically see his brain working, coming to the inevitable conclusion that I was a complete moron and that I had no idea how to date. How had I ever thought I could handle a whole romantic dinner's worth of conversation? I was so much better off on the back of that snowmobile when I couldn't say anything.

"I'm hungry," he said finally. "You hungry?"

My spirits drooped along with my shoulders. "Sure."

"Let's go get some food."

He walked past me then, his boots crunching through the snow, and this time he didn't offer to take my hand.

We rode the snowmobile back down to the resort in silence. The whole way I kept thinking of topics I could chat with him about, trying to figure out how I could get this date back on course. Each subject I came up with, however, sounded lamer than the last, and by the time we got back to civilization, I had exhausted myself. Part of me just wanted to beg out of the eating part of the night and retreat back to my room to lick my wounds. Besides, snagging a table anywhere on the resort property posed all kinds of problems. We could bump into my mother, my brother, any of the Shays. Any of these people could blow my cover in an instant.

Yeah. Bailing seemed like the safest bet for a number of reasons.

"Actually, Connor? I'm kind of tired," I said, once the snowmobile had been safely returned to the garage.

"Really?" His eyebrows shot up. "Because I was going to take you to this burger place I know. We're talking the best cheeseburgers you've ever tasted. They mix the cheese right into the burger. It's like heaven."

My stomach grumbled audibly and we both laughed. He caught my eye and I felt myself start to relax. Maybe this evening *was* salvageable after all.

"I guess I have to do what the stomach commands," I joked.

"Cool," Connor said. "My car's parked just

around the corner."

On the way to the restaurant we talked about school and the courses we'd be taking the following semester. We hadn't signed up for any of the same classes, and Connor had found some interesting ones I hadn't even heard of. Before I knew it we were sitting in a vinyl booth with a pair of plastic menus in front of us and I hadn't said anything even remotely embarrassing. We ordered our burgers and I sat back, filled with the scents of frying onions and oily french fries. The burger place was basically a glorified diner with chrome accents and lots of plastic plants. No one from the resort would ever be caught dead there, except for, possibly, Biff. I was safe.

A brief silence fell. I pulled the ceramic box of sugar packets toward me and started to toy with it. After a couple of torturous seconds, I decided to tap into one of the better topics I'd thought of on the ride down the mountain.

"So, do you like your job at the hotel?" I asked Connor. "I mean, when there aren't a bunch of socialites descending on the place."

"Yeah. I actually do," Connor said, slipping out of his coat. "I like to help people, you know? As long as it's within reason."

"So not ten different kinds of ice," I said.

"Exactly," Connor replied with a laugh. Then he heaved a sigh. "God, I'll be so happy when this wedding is over and they all just go away." His eyes flicked to me. "Except you, of course."

"Well, of course. Not me," I joked in return.

"But I'll get to see you again in a couple of weeks, so I'll have that to get me through," he replied flirtatiously.

I blushed like nobody's business and concentrated on rearranging the sugar packets. Okay. We were officially past the awkward. Maybe I wasn't a total disaster at this dating thing.

"It's just, they have so many events planned," Connor groaned. "Every night a different room is reserved. There's a wine tasting and a rehearsal dinner and a bachelor party and—"

"Oh God. The bachelor party," I said desperately, before I remembered that I really shouldn't. I froze instantly and hoped he'd just let it go by.

"I know. They're so cheesy, right?" he said. "I can only imagine what this one will be like. They're probably flying the entertainment in from Monte Carlo or something."

Gulp. Did I need to fly in special, worldly strippers to entertain the Shay clan? How on earth was I going to pull this thing off? I looked at Connor, who was shaking his head and smiling, and realized that I had a perfect source right here. Connor was a guy, ergo he might actually know what guys would like. It wasn't much of a stretch.

"Have you ever been to a bachelor party?" I asked him with feigned innocence.

"A couple," he said.

Score! "What were they like?"

"Why do you ask?" he said.

"I'm doing a study on the male species for biology class," I said, rolling my eyes.

"Well, okay then. If it's in the name of science," he joked. He sat up straight and leaned forward. "I went to this one for my best friend's brother and it was planned by his future father-in-law. He wanted it to be all sophisticated and stuff, so we went to this fancy steak restaurant in Denver where everything was overpriced and unpronounceable. Every single guy got the filet mignon just because we actually knew what it was, and you could tell the waiter thought we were *so* white trash. Then, every time we got a little loud, they came over and quieted us down like we were kids. It was totally lame and not the groom's thing at all. I mean, when you're throwing a party for a person, you should keep that person's tastes in mind. It's one of the first things they teach you in any hospitality seminar."

Okay, so keep my brother's tastes in mind. No fancy food. No annoying waiters. Have it someplace where we can be loud. Check, check, check, and check.

"So we all thanked the bride's dad at the end of the night, and once he left we went back to my friend's basement and ordered a bunch of pizzas and wings," Connor told me. "That was when it got fun. We had a poker tournament and played video games and everyone got stupid drunk. The groom loved it. When guys get together, they just want to be guys, you know?"

I smiled. He was so down-to-earth. No posturing or trying to sound supercool. Just honest. I liked that.

"So no strippers?" I said.

Connor grimaced. "Strippers are fine, I guess, but you don't *need* 'em. Plus, at the other bachelor party? For my cousin? We got a stripper and it was a big mistake."

"Why?"

"Because the bride's father and brother were there the whole time," Connor said with a shudder. "Let's just say the dad didn't appreciate his future son-in-law getting tied to a chair by some chick with no top on."

Wow. I hadn't even thought of that. Imagine a stripper giving my brother a lap dance or whatever while Mr. Shay and all his fashionable friends looked on? Not a good idea.

"Interesting," I said with a nod. He had no idea how much he had just helped me, and I couldn't even tell him. Luckily the waitress chose that moment to bring our hamburgers.

"I can't imagine what this one's going to be like, though," Connor said, handing me the ketchup. "What do millionaire fashion designers do for a good time? Trade private jets? I bet the groom was born with a silver spoon up his butt."

I felt my face overheat with indignation. "He's not like that," I said. "My br . . . my boss, I mean. The Janssens. They're not as rich as the Shays. I mean, they have money, but not, like, crazy money. They're more low maintenance."

"Right. That's why they have two nannies staying with them at a five-star resort for two weeks," Connor said, shaking some salt onto his fries.

Okay. There was nothing I could say to that. After all, Biff and I had made up and supported that particular lie. It was time to change the subject before we got into dangerous territory.

"So . . . how about those Broncos?" I said hopefully.

And happily, Connor turned out to be just as much of a sports fan as I was.

Chapter 9

The next morning I was still glowing over all the good-night smooching Connor and I had done in the car after we'd returned to the resort, so when my mother stopped by and told me she had made a hair appointment for me, I didn't even protest. She looked amazed as I grabbed my key card and closed the door behind me, all smiles, but she didn't question it. Probably she figured I was sleepwalking and if she woke me up I'd bolt. Of course, half an hour later I was wishing I had done just that.

"I would just feel so much better if you had a date," my mother said, flipping through *Vogue* magazine in the creamy leather chair next to mine. Melena, the woman who was cutting my hair, smirked at me in the mirror and I felt an instant kinship. Even if she was six feet tall, had straight-as-a-pin bangs and perfectly lined eyes.

"I don't see what the big deal is," I told my

mom. "The bride is the center of attention, right? It's not like anyone is going to notice me."

"I beg to differ," my mother said, looking up. She was getting her highlights done so she had four thousand silver foils sticking out all around her head. Quite an appropriate look for Christmas Eve, actually. She could have been an ornament. "You are the sister of the groom. You're going to be in all the pictures . . . at the head table. You're going to *have* to dance at some point, Farrah. How is any of that going to work when you don't have a date? How is it going to look?"

"It's going to look like I don't have a boyfriend right now," I replied tersely.

Melena surreptitiously squeezed my shoulder and I bit my lip to keep from smiling. My mother hated it when I smiled in the middle of conversations she deemed to be serious.

Of course, I wished I could have told my mother that I did sort of have a boyfriend, *so there*. Last night Connor and I had even exchanged cell phone numbers and, even though I still couldn't imagine getting up the guts to call him out of the blue, he was already number four on my speed dial (after 911, Jonah, and Dana). But I couldn't tell my mother that. Because then she would insist on meeting him and not only would she grill him with a thousand inappropriate questions, he would also find out that I was not, in fact, a nanny, but one of the evil wedding-party guests instead.

"Well, haven't you met any nice boys at school?" she implored. "Maybe one of them would like to come. It *is* going to be the event of the year. Surely someone you know would like to attend."

"Mom, I can't just call one of the guys from school and invite them to my brother's wedding," I told her, shifting in my seat. "That's a serious invite. If I do that then whoever I ask will think I like him."

"Well, what's so bad about that?" she asked.

"Mom—"

"I swear, Farrah, you act like having a boyfriend is akin to having leprosy," she said, flipping again.

I caught Melena's eye and we both smiled secretly. "Just another couple of minutes and then I'll blow-dry," she said. And I knew what she meant. Once she turned on the hair dryer, my mother would no longer be able to talk to me. Heaven in the form of a styling tool.

"Oh! I know! What if we fly out one of your high school friends? Surely one of them would be happy to do you a favor," my mother said suddenly.

"Mom! You are not flying out a date for me!" I cried, appalled.

"Why not? What about Duncan? Oh, he would make a lovely date. He's so stylish. I bet he already owns his own tuxedo," she said. "I always thought he had a bit of a crush on you."

"Uh, Duncan came out of the closet the night of graduation and moved to Paris with his boyfriend," I said.

"Oh." My mother's face fell. "Paris would be a bit of an expensive ticket."

I snorted. Had she not heard the part about him being gay? But I guess she didn't need to be bothered admitting she was wrong about his crush.

"Let's think. There must be someone else. We could pay for the airfare and the ride to and from the airport. . . ."

"Mom!" I said loudly. So loudly she startled and the magazine slipped out of her lap, hitting the floor with a thud. My skin was hot as I noticed a few of the other clients shooting me irritated looks.

"What?" she asked, hand to chest.

"You are not flying me out a charity date," I said through my teeth. "Do you have any idea how humiliating that would be?"

"Well, I . . ." She hesitated and I could see that she was taking this in. That she hadn't considered that my feelings might be hurt by her suggestion. Finally she looked around and realized we had an audience. Her eyes softened as she looked at me. "I just want to see you happy, Farrah. That's all."

Well, I thought, *you should have seen me last night, then.*

"What would make me really happy would be if you just dropped the subject," I told her firmly.

Melena put down her scissors, placed a diffuser over her hair dryer, and turned it on, effectively drowning out every voice around me, including my mother's. As far as I was concerned, the stylist was my new best friend.

On Christmas morning, I met my mother, stepfather, and brothers in the beautifully decorated lobby to make the trek out to the Shays' cottage. My mom sat in a shaft of light from one of the windows, checking her face from every conceivable angle in a gold pocket mirror. The boys were dressed in matching white turtlenecks, green sweaters, and brown cords and, in anticipation of presents, were jumping up and down like puppies. At one point, I seriously thought Hunter was going to hyperventilate or possibly start ripping open the fake presents that had been placed around the huge Christmas tree in the center of the lobby, so I gently suggested to my mother that her makeup looked fine and we should just go.

"Why did Santa bring our presents to Marni's house?" Ben asked me, holding my hand as we made our way out the back door of the hotel. The day was crisp and clear and didn't feel quite as cold as the last few. I took a deep breath and savored the mountain air.

"Well, because Marni's cottage has a chimney and you know how Santa loves to go down chimneys," I told him.

"But he doesn't *have* to go down chimneys. Mom said! Lance and Jenna don't have chimneys so he goes in through their window," Ben protested, his brow set in consternation.

My mother clutched her fur collar closer to her neck and shot me an exasperated look, as if I'd just ruined years of careful and clever parenting.

"Farrah didn't say he *needs* a chimney," Jonah corrected, lifting Ben up in both arms and setting him down on his shoulder for a ride. "She said he *loves* chimneys. I think he prefers to use them, but of course, if there isn't one on the house, then he has other ways of getting inside."

Ben thought about this for a while, and the serious face finally fell away. Bless Jonah. The boy was going to be a good father someday.

Ack. Maybe even soon. He was going to be married in just a few days, after all. I felt nearly dizzy at the idea of having nieces and nephews and decided to banish the thought. It was Christmas. I didn't have to think about anything I didn't want to think about.

The Shays were all standing near the door of their cabin to welcome us in from the cold, dressed in holiday-appropriate preppy gear—all reds and pearls and tweed. Their cottage was really more like a mansion and completely decked out for the holiday. Fresh fir garlands were draped along the walls and the staircase, there were poinsettias everywhere, and a huge tree stood in a corner surrounded by so many presents there didn't seem to be any floor left. A fire crackled and popped in the stone fireplace, where velvet stockings bulged with gifts, and a rotund woman in a maid's uniform served up coffee, hot chocolate, and scones. I sunk into one of the leather sofas next to Biff, who was still in her black thermal pj's, texting wildly on her PDA.

"What are you up to?" I asked.

"Texting my friend Lois. We keep each other informed on our gifts in case there's anything we want to trade," Biff said, not looking up from the small screen. "I've already shored up a surfboard and a pair of purple Uggs as long as there's something over there she wants."

She lifted her chin to indicate the pile of gifts. I couldn't imagine there wasn't something in there this Lois girl wouldn't covet. The sheer number of gifts set the odds in her favor.

"Can we get down to the booty already?" Biff asked, dropping her arms at her sides like she was at the end of her rope. Her demand interrupted the parental small talk that was going on over by the kitchen. Jim was trying to smile politely while firmly holding the boys back from massacring the pile of gifts.

"I think that might be a wise idea," he said with a pained smile.

"All right, then!" Mr. Shay announced, clapping his hands together. "Let's see what Santa brought!"

"Yay!"

Jim let the boys go and they practically pounced on the presents.

"Which ones are for me? Which ones are for me?" Hunter kept repeating again and again, his eyes wild as a rabid dog's.

My mother dropped gracefully to her knees and started pulling out the boys' gifts. The Shays each handed one another a box, and Marni came over with a present for Biff. The boys quickly unearthed a set of Legos and begged for it to be opened so they could start building. Jonah took care of that, while my mother laid a box in my lap.

"I think you're really going to like this one," she said with a wink.

I swallowed hard. I dreaded my mother's gifts each year. She was always giving me pink cashmere sweaters or shirts with bows and ruffles or shoes with heels. All of it was still shoved in the back of my closet in Jersey with the tags still on. I always tried to act like I liked the presents, not wanting to spoil Christmas for everyone with an argument, but somehow I felt like it was going to be harder this year, with Biff there and the Shays looking on.

I opened the box slowly and lifted the lid, then said a little prayer for mercy before unfolding the tissue paper. My jaw nearly dropped off my face. Inside was the black and white-patchwork corduroy bag I had admired in one of the store windows when my mother and I had gone shopping the other day. She had told me it looked like something a New York bike messenger would carry and huffed away, leaving me to salivate on my own.

"I can't believe you bought this!" I said, taking the bag out and letting the box fall to the floor.

"Sweet! Your mom has good taste," Biff said.

"Let me know if you want to trade for something later," she added under her breath.

"No way," I replied. It was the first perfect gift my mother had given me in years. I wasn't letting it go for anything.

"Well, Marni and I went down to the shops yesterday and she seemed to think it would be all right for school," my mother told me with a smile.

"Very retro," Marni affirmed.

"As long as you don't think it's a date purse or something," Mom added.

I somehow refrained from rolling my eyes and got up to give her a one-armed hug. "Thanks, Mom. I love it."

Over her shoulder I smiled my thanks to Marni, who grinned in return. Maybe she had changed my brother into a preppy, tennis-playing go-getter, but it seemed her influence on my mother might be a good thing.

"Give her ours! Give her ours!" Jonah said, looking like the sparkly-eyed kid I remembered from our childhood Christmases. Somehow it made me miss my father with a sudden and crippling ache. Not that I was surprised. I always missed my father more on Christmas Day.

"Okay, okay!" Marni replied with a laugh. She swung her perfect blond hair over her shoulder and crouched to the ground. The box she selected was big and bulky but didn't look too heavy from the way she was carrying it. She deposited it on the coffee table in front of me, and I saw her parents exchange a curious glance.

"Wow. That's big," I said.

"I bet it's a Dior coat," Biff said under her breath. "My sister just *loves* to give out Dior coats."

"It's not a Dior coat," my brother said, crossing his arms over his chest.

"Good. Because I don't know what that is," I told him, earning a laugh from the room.

"Well? Open it!"

My face burned under the spotlight as I ripped the paper off the gift. It was a MacBook. A beautiful, sleek laptop. At least, that was what the picture on the box told me.

"No! Freakin'! Way!" I cried, jumping up. "You guys got me a laptop?"

"Yes, we did!" Marni said, clasping her hands together happily.

"We figured you'd need something portable for all your intrepid reporting," Jonah said as I hugged him.

"This is a good model," Mr. Shay commented, putting his glasses on to study the box. "Top of the line. Nice choice."

"Jonah, Marni. That is so generous of you!" my mother said.

"Thanks, you guys! This is incredible," I said, hugging Marni as well.

"I'm glad you like it," Marni replied, squeezing me back.

Mr. Shay produced a Swiss Army knife to help me open the box. I got the feeling he wanted to check it out almost as badly as I did. The boys tore into more toys, while Marni returned to the tree to find more gifts for Biff, her mother, Jonah, and Jim. I noticed that she waited and watched everyone open every present, whether it was from her or not, and saw the joy register in her face when the person liked what they opened. She had yet to search out a gift for herself and seemed interested only in giving to other people.

I looked up at my brother and watched him watch her as well, with a glint of admiration in his eyes. Kind of like the way my dad used to look at my mom. I felt my heart swell and thought of the good old Grinch's heart swelling up and breaking the heart-measuring device. Maybe this wedding wasn't such a bad idea after all. I almost wished Connor could see Marni just then, the way Jonah and I were seeing her. He couldn't think that she and her family were *all* bad if he saw this.

"Yes! A Razr phone," Biff said suddenly, holding up a small box. "And it's pink. Lois is going to *love* this."

Biff's parents chuckled, and I suddenly felt the weight of my own phone in the pocket of my jeans. I wondered what Connor was doing just then. What his house was like on Christmas morning. Would he call me today to wish me a Merry Christmas? I placed my hand over my phone and wished for it. A call from my possible boyfriend would put the cherry on top of what was already turning out to be one of the best Christmases in recent history.

"Ugh! I am totally staying in your room tonight," Biff said, rubbing her stomach as we tromped down the hallway. "Otherwise you're gonna have to roll me and my gut back up the hill."

"That was one humongous dinner," I agreed.

The Shays had thrown a Christmas banquet in the main ballroom and all the guests that had flown in early for the wedding had attended. There were carolers in traditional colonial garb, glittering Christmas trees all around the room, and a special appearance by a classic storybook Santa Claus, who had handed out five-hundred-dollar gift certificates to the Shay flagship store in New York. My head felt foggy from all the food and candlelight and the one glass of wine my mother had allowed me to drink. That had, at least, taken the edge off the sudden fear I'd developed that Connor would be working the party and would see me there, all dressed up in my new skirt and red top, hobnobbing with the enemy. But the fear had never been realized. Whatever Connor was doing with his holiday, he didn't appear to be doing it at the River Lodge.

My eyes at half-mast, I missed the slot for the key card three times before finally managing to open the door. Biff walked right in and collapsed face-first on the extra queen-size bed in my room. She kicked off her leopard-print flats and stayed there, her head buried in a pillow. I half expected her to start snoring right then.

As a habit, I flipped on *SportsCenter*. Even on Christmas Day the ESPN crew had something to report. I reached for my phone, which I had left on the nightstand, not wanting to be one of those girls who pathetically checked for messages every five seconds all through dinner. Before looking at the screen, I closed my eyes and told myself it was all right if he hadn't called. Who knew what he was doing today? He hadn't mentioned anything. For all I knew he could be driving his whole family across the state and back to visit some relative. He could be crazy busy. He didn't *have* to call me.

I took a deep breath and looked at the screen. No messages.

"Dammit," I said, flopping back on my enormous, puffy pillows.

"Whassa matter?" Biff asked. She managed to turn her head toward me, but kept her cheek to the mattress.

"Connor still hasn't called," I replied, tossing the phone toward the foot of the bed. I felt like an idiot. It wasn't as if any guy had ever called me on Christmas before. Why did I expect this one to be any different?

Possibly because he was the first one to ever make out with you and not insult you afterward? I thought.

"So? Call him," Biff told me. She rubbed her nose back and forth on her arm, dealing with an itch. "You do have his number, right?"

My full stomach churned at the very idea of calling Connor. What if he didn't want to talk to me? What if he didn't think of him and me as the kind of relationship where one called the other on religious holidays? What if he was in the middle of a family thing and rushed me off the phone? What if we had one of those conversations where it was all dead air? To be honest, I had never been great at carrying on phone conversations and never quite understood why so many girls my age seemed to have their cells permanently attached to their ears. I didn't think I could handle the awkwardness of a stilted phone convo with Connor.

"I don't know . . ." I said, only because she was still staring at me.

"Well, you want to talk to him, right?" she said. "I say, if you want to talk to somebody, call them. This is the twenty-first freaking century, after all."

She was right. She was. I mean, I was a strong, confident woman. I could call a guy. I lifted my head off the pillow and sat up straight to reach for the phone. My heart was pounding so hard you'd think I was considering calling the president. But Connor was just a guy. Just a guy who had kissed me on two separate occasions. A guy who didn't want to hear from a girl didn't kiss that girl, right? I mean, it wasn't like I was going to call him and he was going to not know who I was.

Oh God. What if it took him a second to remember who I was?

Right then, there was a knock on the door that nearly scared me out of my skin. I looked at Biff, who managed to lift her head high enough to rest it on the back of her hand.

"If that's someone with food, tell them to go away," she groaned. Then her eyes popped open wide. "Unless they have that cake from the first night. I could always choke some of that down."

I rolled my eyes at her and opened the door. My knees nearly buckled. It was Connor. He stood in front of me in a white turtleneck sweater with his blond hair perfectly tousled. Hot Connor all the way.

"Merry Christmas, Jane," he said with a smile. And he produced a gift from behind his back.

Well. Guess he did remember who I was.

Chapter 10

There was no moving Biff, so Connor and I decided to go down to the huge porch off the lobby, which overlooked the bunny slopes and the cottages beyond. Jingle bells were strung all along the railing, and mistletoe hung from the eaves. Rustic lanterns flickered on the various tables, surrounded by sprigs of red berries and green plaid bows. There were a few other couples sitting out enjoying the view, but I chose a quiet pair of chairs toward the end so that we could have some privacy. I bundled up in my coat and scarf and sat on one of the big wooden rocking chairs, while Connor went back inside to order up a couple of hot teas from the café. I couldn't stop staring at the wrapped gift sitting on the table next to me, next to the flickering lantern.

Connor had bought me a present. He had shopped and chosen something and wrapped it and made a special trip to bring it to me. I felt pleasantly warm and tingly just thinking about it. All day long I had been dreading the idea that he wasn't thinking of me as seriously as I was thinking of him, but instead, he'd been a step ahead of me all along. I hadn't gotten him anything. Hadn't even considered it. Which, of course, made me feel as guilty as sin.

"Hey. I got peppermint tea," Connor said, returning with two steaming cups. "Seemed occasion-appropriate."

"Thanks."

I sat up and reached for the cup with both hands. "I can't believe you got me a present. I feel so bad," I said, averting my eyes.

"It's nothing big, I swear," he told me as he sat down in the next rocker. "I just saw it and I thought you might like it."

My face flushed at the idea of him thinking about what I might like. I took a sip of my tea and gazed up at the stars. I wanted to remember this feeling for as long as humanly possible. Feeling like someone I liked actually liked me back. And a perfect someone at that.

"So, are you going to open it?" he asked.

"Don't have to ask me twice," I said giddily.

I put down my teacup and grabbed the gift. It was heavy for its size. Connor watched me expectantly as I shredded the paper. I lifted the lid off the green box and found a beautiful, brown suede journal inside. The scent of the leather mixed with the peppermint tea was intoxicating. Or maybe it was the way Connor was studying me. Like he didn't want to miss a second of my reaction.

"Wow! Connor!" I breathed. "It's amazing."

I took the book out and ran my hand over the buttery cover, then flipped through the blank pages. They were made of heavy stock and a bit frayed at the edges, purposely antiqued.

"You like it?" he asked, leaning forward in his chair. "I figured since you were a writer and all . . ."

"I love it," I told him honestly. "I actually used to keep a journal in high school, but I . . ."

"What?" he asked.

"I stopped," I told him, my skin going prickly. "I don't know why."

That was a total lie. I'd stopped after the Tommy McNabb incident, because so much of the journals up until then had focused on my undying obsession with him—how excited I was whenever he talked to me, verbatim accounts of what he'd said, descriptions of his smile, his hair, his clothes. After our night in the closet, the very thought of those journals was humiliating and I'd given up entirely. But that had been a few years ago now, and good things were happening again. Things that I just might want to look back on and read about later.

"But I've wanted to start again," I told him, brightening. "This is the perfect gift."

"I'm glad you like it," Connor said with a smile. He reached out his hand for mine and gently tugged me out of my chair. "C'mere."

I couldn't stop grinning as we walked over to the log railing. Connor put his arm around me and we huddled together against a cold breeze, looking up at the stars. I took a deep breath and sighed.

"I'm glad you came," I said lightly, without even thinking it through first. Of course, the moment it was out, I was embarrassed worried that I'd said too much.

"Me, too," he said, pulling me a bit closer. "I still can't believe you're actually staying here. That night when I found you in the kitchen, I thought I was hallucinating."

"I know. So did I," I said.

He stared into my eyes, like he was trying to find something there. "I wanted to ask you out all semester," he said seriously.

My heart flip-flopped. "You're kidding."

There was no way. There was absolutely no

way that out of all the people in our class, Connor had noticed me. I mean, he could admire my writing in the newspaper, that I could maybe comprehend, but why would he want to ask me out?

"No. I'm totally serious. I just never knew what to say," he told me. "You're kind of intimidating, you know?"

"I'm intimidating? Please!"

"No! You are! You're smart, for one, and you're not giggly and flirty like other girls. With them, it's like, if they flip their hair or whatever, you know they want you to ask them out. But you don't do any of that stuff."

I looked down, embarrassed. Somehow everything always came back to me not being girly.

"Whenever you looked at me, you looked so serious," he continued. "I always kind of thought that you thought I was a doofus. And then I nearly killed you with my bike. . . ."

He groaned, as if the very memory of that day was painful to him. I had to smirk at that one. His nearly running me over had been the highlight of my semester.

"I never thought you were a doofus," I said quietly, still nursing the hurt over the idea that I was so unfeminine. I knew he hadn't meant it as an insult, so I was trying to shove it aside.

"So what *did* you think of me?" he asked.

"I thought . . . I thought I really *wanted* you to ask me out," I told him. Even with his confession, I somehow felt that I was going out on a limb as I said this.

His eyes widened. "No way."

"Um, yeah way," I replied with a laugh.

Connor cracked up. "Wow. We're really a couple of idiots, huh?"

"You could say that."

He looked out at the trees and smiled to himself.

"What?" I asked.

"Nothing. If I tell you what I just thought, you really will think I'm a doofus," he said.

"We need to stop using that word." I hesitated a moment, then reached out and laid my hand on his arm. "Come on. Tell me."

After taking a deep breath, he contemplated me for a long moment. Then he shook his head, like he was so going to regret doing this. "All right, well, I was just thinking that it's sort of like fate that we're together now."

"Fate."

"Yeah, well, think about it. English Literature is a required course. There are at least twenty sections of that class, but we get put in the same one," he

149

said, warming to his topic. "Then, when that doesn't get either of us moving, I almost run you over. And when that doesn't work, I end up being the one to catch you and Biff hiding out in the kitchen that first night. Do you know what the chances are of that happening?"

A smile twitched at my lips. "Slim to none?"

"Slim to none." His eyes caught mine, and my heart responded with an extra-large thump. "Somebody's trying to tell us something."

"Well, whoever they are, I like them," I replied.

Connor smiled. As he leaned in to kiss me, my breath caught in my throat. I hoped that the bit of peppermint tea I'd swallowed had neutralized the wine on my breath. The last thing I needed was for severe stinky mouth to harpoon this perfectly romantic moment. His lips were just about to touch mine when, down below the balcony, I saw something move. In the next moment, Marni and Jonah stepped into view, strolling hand in hand through the snow. My heart lurched and I sprung back, but it was too late. My brother had looked up and for a split second, our eyes had locked. It was long enough for me to see the total confusion and surprise on his face. I had told my brother there was a guy named Connor at school that I liked, but

I had failed to mention that said guy worked at the River Lodge.

"What's the matter?" Connor asked me as I backed quickly away from the railing.

"I just . . . I don't feel so well all of a sudden," I told him. "I think I ate too much at dinner."

I was dying to look back over the railing, to see if my brother was still there or if he was coming up here to grill me. But if I looked again, Connor would definitely get suspicious. I had to get out of there, fast. No. I had to get *both* of us out of there. Because if Jonah did come up here and find Connor alone, he and Marni would still give him the third degree. They were both so overly friendly and curious it sort of negated any thoughts of discretion.

"Where's the bathroom?" I asked, looking around wildly.

I couldn't believe this was happening. I'd just obliterated our romantic Christmas and now I was going to have to leave him with the impression of me on a vomit run.

Oh, what a tangled web we weave . . .

"It's around the corner, past the café," Connor replied.

"Show me," I said, grabbing his arm.

He let out a startled noise as he tripped forward,

but managed to grab my gift as I dragged him back inside. A few of the posh, fur-and-suede-ensconced guests shot us disturbed looks as we sprinted through the lobby, but I barely even noticed. Every moment I felt like an elevator would ping and my brother and Marni would snag us. Every second I saw them coming across the lobby on a mission for information. But somehow, I made it to the bathroom safely and shoved my way through the door.

"I'll be right here!" Connor called after me.

I raced inside, locked myself into a stall, and wondered how long, exactly, I had to stay there to make it seem like I had gotten sick, but not violently, grossly, nonstop sick. I pressed my forehead against the cool surface of the stall door and took a deep breath, resolving to count to a hundred Mississippis. By then, Jonah would have given up looking for me—if he *was* looking for me—and I could claim that it was a false alarm and I felt much better.

Then, tomorrow, I was just going to have to avoid my brother for as long as possible—at least long enough for me to figure out what I was going to tell him.

"Thanks for coming in," Emily Szabo said, tucking her pencil skirt beneath her as she sat down in her ergonomic chair. "I nearly panicked when I looked at my calendar and realized that I hadn't done one thing for the bachelor party. Imagine my surprise when I asked who my contact was and found out it was you."

I shifted uncomfortably in my chair. "Bad surprise?" I asked.

"Are you kidding? Good surprise," Emily said. "I dread bachelor parties, mostly because the best men that I deal with are total Neanderthals. I already like your brother that much more for choosing you."

"Um . . . I should tell you, I have no idea how I'm going to pay for this," I said, feeling like a loser.

Emily waved me off. "Oh, please, it's already been budgeted into the overall cost of the wedding." She hit a few buttons on her keyboard and her eyes widened. "In fact, we have quite an ample budget for this particular night, so we can do pretty much anything you want."

Emily smiled at me over her glass-topped desk. She had wavy black hair pinned back in a loose bun and wore a chic black suit and white top, the kind of outfit you'd expect to see on a Manhattanite businesswoman, but I guess that's the kind of image one has to project as the party planner for one of the top resorts in the country. The wall behind her desk was practically papered with framed photos of her posing with celebrities. Movie stars, professional athletes, politicians, fashion designers. It seemed as if she had worked with everyone who was anyone. And now she was meeting with little old Farrah Jane Morris of the Bergen County Morrises and I was thoroughly intimidated. But then I remembered how Connor had thought *I* was intimidating once, and I resolved to speak my mind. If I could really do anything I wanted, then I was going to throw my brother the party *he* wanted, even if I had to face down this woman and her crudités platters to do it.

"Okay, I was thinking . . . my brother and his friends love video games. Always have," I said, sitting up straight. "So maybe we could set up a bunch of TVs with video consoles. They could have a tournament or something. These guys *love* their tournaments."

I expected Emily to laugh or throw me out, but instead she started taking notes.

"All right, how many people do you expect to attend?" she asked.

I did a quick mental count. "Well, my brother has his three best friends from high school and there are about six or seven other college buddies that are coming to the wedding. Plus Marni's dad,

I guess. I don't know. Do you think the Shays will want anyone else to come?"

"You're the hostess. You get to decide who to invite," Emily said.

I must have looked petrified. At least that was how I felt at the idea of making such a decision. And Emily noticed.

"Who would your brother want there?" she asked gently.

"He'd probably want to keep it small. You know, celebrate with the guys."

"Then that's what you should do," she told me.

I smiled. "Okay, then. Let's say thirteen including me and my brother."

"Good. You'll want to come up with some kind of invitation. Something we can leave in their rooms," Emily said. "Or I can do that for you, if you like."

"I think I can handle that," I told her.

"All right. What about food? Anything specific you had in mind?" she asked.

I cleared my throat. "He likes pan pizzas. Oh! And buffalo chicken wings—really spicy. Oh! And can we get grilled cheese sandwiches?"

Now Emily did laugh, but it was a nice laugh. "I like your enthusiasm."

"You can do it?" I asked.

"I think we can handle grilled cheese," she said, nodding as she made some more notes.

"Cool. That would be so cool," I said, starting to relax. "My brother practically lives for grilled cheese."

Emily eyed me for a long moment and then, finally, smiled. "I like your style."

"You do?" I asked, sitting up a bit straighter.

"Are you kidding?" She typed a few things into her computer and made another note on a pad in front of her. "Most of the people that come through here insist on sushi or a Thai buffet or something equally high maintenance. This party is going to be more fun to plan than anything I've worked on in the last year."

"Cool," I said with a grin. "So what about the video game thing?"

"That should be no problem," she replied. "We have a deal with the Bose store in town. We should be able to get a few big screens and a bunch of games on loan. They supplied all the equipment for Elway's Super Bowl party last year."

I suddenly felt faint. "John Elway had his Super Bowl party here last year?"

"Ooops," Emily said, her cheeks going pink. "I'm not supposed to divulge things like that. But now that you know, he did, and it was incredible.

He's booked us again this year, but you didn't hear it from me."

"Wow." I was already plotting how to get back here on Super Bowl Sunday to get myself some autographs. "Well, then. If you're good enough for Elway, you're definitely good enough for us."

Emily smiled and stood up to shake my hand. "If you think of anything else, let me know."

"I will," I replied happily.

I walked out of her office feeling very accomplished and mature. I couldn't believe that just a couple of days ago I was nervous about the bachelor party. Now it was all under control. Things were definitely looking up.

Then, halfway down the hall, Biff appeared out of nowhere and pulled me into a hallway with nothing but phones and a water cooler.

"My sister and your brother are on the prowl," she whispered, out of breath.

My heart constricted. "They're looking for me?"

"They're *dying* to know who the guy is you were with last night," she said. "Marni's all set to make space for him at our table."

"Oh God." I hid my face in my hands. "What did you tell them?"

"I told them they must have been so high on

love they hallucinated," she said. "And that you were spending the whole morning working on the bachelor party so they'd better leave you alone."

"Huh. You're good."

"Tell me something I don't know," she replied. "But if I were you, I'd make myself scarce. Go get your stuff and we can hang out at the top of the mountain or something."

"Got it," I said. "I'll meet you by the lifts in fifteen."

Biff checked her watch and nodded. "Be there."

We parted and I made my way through the lobby to the elevators, checking over my shoulder every couple of seconds. Every blonde I saw sent me into panic mode, but none of them turned out to be Marni. I made it all the way up to my floor without incident and was almost at the door to my room, when a door across the hall opened and I nearly jumped out of my skin.

"Psssst! Jane! In here!"

Once I had assured myself that I was not having a coronary, I registered that Connor was sticking his head out of the room across the way.

"What are you doing?" I asked.

"You have to see this." He grinned mischievously. Which was perfectly impossible to resist.

"See what?"

He reached his arm out and pulled me into the strange room. The curtains were drawn almost all the way closed, letting just a sliver of light through. I couldn't see much beyond the entryway.

"Okay, whose room is this? What're we doing?" I asked.

"First things first," he said, tucking my hair behind my ear. It sprang right back again, of course, but it was the thought that counted. "I just went by your room to see if you were okay. Where were you?"

"Oh, just . . . dropping the boys off for ski lessons," I lied. I had, in fact, done that, but I had done it two hours earlier.

"So you're feeling better?" he asked.

"Definitely," I replied.

"Good. Then I can finally do this."

He grabbed me up in a kiss so fast, I didn't even have time to react. Before I knew it I was pressed back against the wall, out of breath, as he touched his tongue to mine. Then a door slammed in the hallway and he jumped back, leaving me swooning.

"Sorry. Just couldn't help myself," he said with a smile that made me blush.

"Umm . . . so, where are we exactly?" I asked.

"Right. You have to see this." He took my hand and pulled me away from the wall. "I was sent up here to remove the minibar from this room."

"Someone asked you to remove the minibar? Can you even do—"

My sentence never got the chance to finish itself. I was too stunned by the state of the room before me. A hand truck stood in the center of the room, for removing the minibar, I supposed. The king-size bed, which I would have thought immovable, was shoved into a corner. All the other furniture was lined up on the walls with chair seats facing away from the room, making it impossible to sit in them without moving them. But the furniture wasn't what made me pause. It was the sheer amount of stuff. There were shopping bags and boxes everywhere—on the desk, atop the dresser, piled up on the floor. A stack of workout DVDs sat next to the television next to a pair of dumbbells and a resistance band. A tower of shoe boxes tilted precariously near the window, and a mountain of purses, scarves, and shoes took up most of the space at the foot of the bed. Dresses, sweaters, ponchos, jackets, and slacks jammed the open closet and hung from the door of the TV armoire, from the wall sconce, even from the fire sprinkler.

"Yeah, that's a safety violation," Connor said, pointing it out. "But it gets better."

He dragged me into the bathroom. Every inch of space on the counter around the sink was occupied by pots of creams and salves, trays of eye makeup and lip liner. There were tools I didn't even recognize and dozens of brushes and pencils. Sitting atop a plastic box were two nude-colored blobs that looked like breast implants, and there was a tiered tray with six different pairs of false eyelashes, one of them decorated with rhinestones. In the shower were eight bottles of shampoo and conditioner and another half dozen body washes.

"Okay, who lives here? A drag queen?" I asked.

"Better." Connor picked up one of the false-eyelash trays and brought it close to inspect it. "One of the bridesmaids," he said gleefully.

My breath left me. I wasn't sure whether I was intrigued or appalled. Those girls were pretty and well dressed, no doubt, but who needed this much stuff?

"Which one?" I asked.

"Some ridiculously skinny girl with big eyes and brown hair," he said. Carina. Had to be. She probably felt like she needed all this stuff to keep up with Calista. "Apparently she's on a perpetual diet and she can't resist the temptation of the mini-bar. God forbid she have a little self-control."

"Seriously," I said.

"Can you believe all this stuff?" Connor asked, picking up one of the creams now. "What the hell is microdermabrasion anyway? Sounds like some kind of self-torture."

I opened my mouth to answer—well, to tell him I had no idea—but he cut me off.

"Not that you'd know," he said with a laugh, dropping the pot back on the counter.

I felt like I had just been slapped. Right. Of course. Uncoiffed, mannish, antifeminine me wouldn't have a clue what microdermabrasion was. Okay, so I didn't, but he didn't have to act like it was such a foregone conclusion.

"I bet you don't have any of this stuff in *your* room," he continued, his eyes dancing.

Was he mocking me? Was I so unpretty that it was blatantly clear I wasn't even trying? Visions of Tommy McNabb's smirking face, still flushed from our kisses, danced through my head. My insides felt sour and squishy and I found myself backing out of the room.

"I have to go," I said.

Connor's face fell. "Are you okay? You look pale."

Probably because of my total lack of makeup.

"I'm fine," I said. "I just . . . I'm supposed to meet Biff."

"You should stay in, though, if you're not feeling well again," he said.

"No. I'm fine," I told him, gunning for the door. In fact, I felt more like I was going to throw up now than I had at any point last night, but he didn't need to know that. "I just have to go."

I tried to ignore the look of confusion on his face as I walked out the door and let it slam.

Chapter 11

"Why, exactly, are we having a secret meeting at Jenna Reggino's cabin?" I asked, huddling farther into my coat. Biff and I had spent the day on the slopes under the sun as she tried—and failed miserably—to teach me how to snowboard. But since then the wind had picked up, and once the sun had gone down, the temperature had plummeted. It was so cold I felt like my eyes were going to freeze in their sockets.

"Who knows?" Biff said. "They're probably planning something for the wedding day. Maybe they're hiring a pink elephant to carry Marni down the aisle or something."

Pink did seem to be these girls' color of choice. When I'd returned to my room that evening I'd found a gift wrapped in pink paper and note on pink stationery, inviting me to a secret meeting of the bridesmaids that night. The paper itself had smelled like roses, and the gift had turned out to be a pink cashmere scarf and matching hat, along with a bottle of rose-scented perfume, none of which I was currently wearing. Apparently Marni's friends had yet to accept the fact that I was not, in fact, a bridesmaid. At first I was just going to ignore the invite, but then Biff had twisted my arm saying I had to be her wingman. Far be it from me to turn down the girl who had played wingman for me ever since the day we met.

But as we made our way toward Jenna's cabin, I dreaded what lay ahead. The last thing I wanted to do was spend time with Carina right now, not after violating her privacy, and especially not now that I knew how very far her Calista obsession reached. I wasn't even sure I was going to be able to look at her without giving away what I knew. And I wasn't exactly psyched to spend an evening with Calista, either.

Biff turned up the walkway to Jenna's cottage. About ten feet from the front door, she stopped suddenly and grabbed my arm.

"Oh, no," she said.

I looked up at the cottage. All the lights appeared to be on and I could hear music playing inside, but I had no idea what had set her off.

"What?" I asked.

"Run!"

Biff turned to sprint, but the front door opened at that very moment and Jenna, Calista, and Carina poured out onto the front step. They were all wearing sparkly clubbing outfits, pink feather boas, and tiaras, and each had a colorful drink in her hand.

"Hey there, girls! Welcome to the party!" Jenna trilled, teetering toward us in her high heels. "Don't even think about trying to bail."

"You didn't tell me this was a bachelorette party! I'm the maid of honor! I'm supposed to throw this!" Biff cried.

"Right. And we knew you never would," Calista said snottily. "Therefore, the ambush."

Jenna slung her arm over Biff's shoulder and forcibly dragged her back toward the cottage. Biff did her best to resist, but Jenna was pretty buff and seemed to have a grip of steel. Either she did *a lot* of Pilates at one of those swank city gyms or maybe the rumors about her former teamster dad and his family were true and their habits had rubbed off.

"Save yourself," Biff choked.

I thought about bolting, figuring none of these girls would have the gall to strong-arm me—a girl they barely knew. But then Marni appeared at the door. Her tiara was larger than the others and she wore a sash across her dress that read BRIDE TO BE.

"You're here!" she said happily as she approached. "I know. Bachelorette parties are such clichés," she said, squeezing my hand. "But I'd love it if you'd stay."

There was nothing on earth I'd like to do less. But it wasn't like I was going to walk away now.

"What kind of honorary bridesmaid would I be if I didn't?" I said, trying to sound chipper.

"Whoo-hoo!" Carina and Jenna cheered.

Calista shot them an irritated look, like they were just *so* immature, and headed inside. Carina ducked her head and quickly followed.

"So . . . my little sister-in-law, who was that boy we saw you getting all cozy with last night?" Marni asked, slipping her arm around mine as we headed up the stairs.

Wow. She wasted no time, did she? I glanced over my shoulder, checking the escape route one last time.

"Uh . . . boy? What boy?" I asked.

Marni gave me a knowing look that told me there was no way she was going to drop this, then led me inside. I had a feeling this was going to be a very long night.

* * *

There were penises everywhere. Chocolate ones, plastic ones, blow-up ones, poster-size ones. They'd been made into whistles, drinking straws, lollipops, earrings. There was even a penis hat circulating and everyone was having their picture taken wearing it. I had never been so grossed out in my life, and I had once watched my brother eat an entire package of bacon in one sitting. I would have thought that this insanely fashionable, sophisticated group would have shied away from the cheesy clichés of bachelorette parties, but apparently it was cool to be cheesy—as long as you went completely over the top with it. At least that was how Jenna explained it to me tipsily as she toyed with a penis-shaped balloon.

Somewhere in the course of the night, the dozen or so girls in attendance changed into baby-doll pajamas and nighties, and powered up the karaoke machine. Thankfully they hadn't thought to bring extra pj's for me and Biff, so we got to stay fully clothed as we watched them slur and stumble their way through "Hollaback Girl" and "Since U Been Gone."

I have to admit, I ended up having a good time. Marni had dropped the Connor-related inquisition early on, distracted by the pink drinks her friends were practically pouring down her throat, so I had temporarily dodged that bullet. If nothing else, watching the wedding party's drunken song-and-dance routines was good for a laugh. Plus, most of Marni's friends turned out to be nice people. Except Calista, of course. She spent the entire night ignoring me and keeping a watchful eye on Biff. There was definitely no love lost between those two.

"Omigod! You must think we're such a bunch of losers!" Carina trilled, dropping down on the couch next to me after finishing a duet of "Material Girl" with Calista.

"No. I don't," I replied. I tried not to stare at her. Were those eyelashes fake or real? Was she wearing those false breast things under her nightie?

Carina poured herself a seltzer and sat back. Her cheeks reddened when she looked at me. "You're checking out my cleavage, aren't you?"

"What? No! No. I just . . . like your night-gown," I improvised.

"It's okay," she said, crossing her arms over her chest. "I know, they're the incredible disappearing boobies."

I laughed and took a sip of my soda.

"I've been wearing inserts lately. You know, in my bra?" she said, lowering her voice.

Oh, I knew. I'd already seen them in the fake flesh. I felt nearly sick with guilt.

"I'm thinking about getting implants, so I've been sort of taking them out for a test spin. But you can't wear them under an outfit like this."

"Oh," I said. I looked away. The very idea of plastic surgery has always given me the heebie-jeebies, but I barely knew the girl. Who was I to judge?

"You don't approve," she said neutrally.

"It's not really my business," I said.

"No, but I'm curious, you know, what other women think," Carina said, touching my leg. "It's a big decision, so . . . why don't you approve?" I looked at her. There was no way this conversation could go well, but I couldn't think of a way out of it. A few feet away, Marni and a now-drunk Biff sang "Sisters Are Doing It for Themselves" at the top of their lungs while the rest of the guests cheered them on.

I took a deep breath and sighed. "It's just, you're gorgeous."

"Yeah right." Carina scoffed and took a sip of her drink.

"You are!" I said, my face heating up with what felt like anger. "You have a great body. I don't understand why you'd want to go through all that pain to fix something that isn't broken."

Carina was silent for a long moment. I figured I must have insulted her, but I wasn't sure how. All I was doing was telling her how great she was.

"I don't know. I figure maybe they'll make me feel more . . . confident," she said. "You know, more womanly. Like . . ."

She trailed off, looking at her friends. Looking at one of them specifically. One who was holding her nose so far in the air she could have caught a 747 in each nostril.

"Like Calista," I said.

"No," she said automatically. "Not necessarily."

But I knew that was what she was thinking. She couldn't take her eyes off the girl. What was the obsession with her friend?

"Carina, Calista isn't the be-all and end-all," I said under my breath. "The girl is mean, for one, which you are clearly not. Plus she's, like, washed up at the age of twenty-three."

"Omigod! You did not just say that!" Carina protested, her eyes wide.

"Look, I know she's your friend, I just . . . She's not all that. That's all," I said, hoping she wasn't about to make a scene.

But instead, she sighed again and slumped. "Try telling my parents that."

"Your parents?"

"They *love* Calista," Carina said, only glancing up for a split second to roll her eyes. "My whole life it's been like 'Why don't you take up modeling, like Calista? Why don't you go to acting classes with Calista?' My mother used to take my books away from me and have me walk around with them on my head instead of letting me read them. I swear my mother wished she would find out one day that Calista and I were switched at birth."

Oh my God. Now we were getting to it. No wonder she was such a basket case. Her parents were evil. I thought I had a hard time dealing with *my* mother's expectations? Imagine being constantly compared to your famous best friend.

I had no idea what to say. Part of me wanted to shake her and tell her to snap out of it, but she'd probably think I was insane. Kind of the way I'd felt that night Biff had accused me of being one of those hot girls who doesn't know she's hot, but worse.

"Man. Parents really can mess with your brain," I heard myself say.

"What?" Carina asked.

"Nothing," I said.

"Who wants to go next?" Marni cried, holding up the microphone as the applause of the group started to die down.

I glanced at Carina, my heart suddenly pounding. "We will!" I shouted, standing.

"We will?" Carina asked.

"Yeah. I have the perfect song for us," I said, taking her hand and pulling her up. She yelped in surprise and half her drink sloshed out of her glass as she placed it down on the coffee table.

I handed Carina a microphone and flipped through the list of songs until I found what I was looking for. My throat was dry as desert air as I punched the numbers into the machine, but I had to do this. We both had to do this. Biff and Marni settled in front and center to watch, and all the rest of the girls started to chant.

"Sing! Sing! Sing!" they said as they clapped their hands. "Sing! Sing! Sing!"

"Omigod! We're not singing that!" Carina cried, laughing as the name of the song popped up on the screen.

"Oh, yes we are," I said.

Carina grinned at me and together we launched into the lyrics of "I'm Too Sexy."

"I'm too sexy for my shirt, so sexy it hurts!" I sang badly.

"Yeah, baby! Sing it!" Biff cried, throwing her arms up.

"And I'm too sexy for Milan, too sexy for

Milan, New York, and Japan!" Carina added, rolling her shoulder back to strike a pose.

The crowd whooped and hollered. Everyone laughed hysterically as we hammed it up and pretended to model and made sexy faces. And by the end Carina and I were doubled over laughing and hugging and I really did feel sexy.

"All right, so we've got all the video games picked out. I ordered a dozen different beers off the hotel's menu and there's gonna be an open bar for four hours," I said, checking off my list in the lobby café the next morning. "What else?"

"What about favors? Have you thought about favors?" Biff asked me, nursing a cup of coffee. There were dark circles under her eyes and she wore her most shape-free outfit yet, a gray sweatshirt, plain jeans, and black boots.

"I have to have favors?" I asked. "What is this, a six-year-old's birthday party?"

"We gave out walkie-talkies at our birthday," Ben announced.

At the other end of the table, Hunter and Ben played a game of kid's Monopoly with utter concentration. Even when Ben spoke, he never took his eyes off the board. I couldn't believe how well behaved they were this morning, and I was grateful for it. If they acted like their usual selves, Biff's hangover would only be exacerbated.

"I know. Your friends loved those," I said. I remembered it well because they had all freaked out when there were no batteries and I'd had to run to the store to buy them.

"Dude, it's all about the favors," Biff told me. "Bachelor parties mean monogrammed flasks or shot glasses or cigars or something."

"Monogrammed flasks? I don't have time to deal with that," I said, feeling suddenly tense. "I don't even know for sure who's coming to this thing."

"Relax," Biff said, lifting a hand to her head. "You're getting a little shrill."

"Forget it. I can't do favors," I said. "It's too late."

"Farrah, you cannot disrespect the time-honored tradition of ridiculously overpriced parting gifts," Biff said. "It's what my people live for."

"Well, actually, not all that many of *your* people are invited," I said.

"What? You're kidding. Did you invite my cousins?" Biff asked. "You have to invite my cousins. My mother will freak."

I was about to sink into despair when Connor appeared at the doorway. My pulse quickened at the sight of him, but it was instantly tempered when I recalled what we had done the last time I'd seen him. I had felt bad enough about invading Carina's privacy, but now that I knew better where Carina got her neurosis, I felt even worse about the whole thing. And as for the other thing, the fact that he'd implied I was no beauty expert, well, that I was not going to think about.

"Hey! Spider-Man and Wolverine! How're my two favorite superheroes?" he asked, coming over to greet the boys.

"Good," Hunter said, distracted.

"Good," Ben echoed.

Connor looked confused. "Okay. What are they on?" he joked, kissing the top of my head.

"It's the spirit of competition," I told him, forcing a smile. "A strong drug."

"Very true. Hey, Biff. How's it going?" he asked.

Biff grunted and waved.

"Oooh. Long night?" Connor pulled up a chair, turned it around, and straddled it. "Well, I've got something that'll cheer you up. Did you tell her what we found in that girl's room?" he asked me.

My heart squeezed, but Biff looked intrigued. She even managed to straighten up more than she had all morning.

"What girl's room?" she asked.

"She didn't tell you?" Connor said gleefully.

"It wasn't that big a deal," I said.

"What are you talking about? It was like a house of horrors in there," Connor said. He turned his chair toward Biff, sensing the willing audience. "Okay, so I get called to this girl's room to remove the minibar—"

"Carina, right?" Biff said, brightening even more.

"Yeah. How did you know?" Connor asked.

Biff shrugged. "I eavesdrop. A lot."

"Right. Well, anyway, I go in there and the place is a huge mess of clothes and shoes and makeup and fake everything. Fake eyelashes, colored contacts, fake . . . you know . . ." He blushed and Biff looked at me.

"She had gel inserts. You know. For her bra," I said.

Biff snorted a laugh and slapped her hand over her mouth. "Why doesn't she just get them done? It's not like she doesn't have the money."

I swallowed hard, trying not to think about my conversation with Carina the night before.

"I wouldn't be surprised if she'd already had tons of stuff done," Connor said. "Girl is clearly whacked in the head."

"Can we talk about something else?" I interjected, my voice sounding strained.

"What's the matter? You look green," Biff said.

"I'm fine. It's just . . . the whole plastic surgery thing," I said. "I don't want to think about it." I cringed for effect, like I was one of those girls who can't even think about blood without fainting. I felt like a total fraud, but it worked. Connor put his hand gently on my back.

"Sorry. We can change the subject," he said.

I sighed, relieved. "Thank you."

"So, what are you writing?" Connor asked, leaning over my shoulder.

I covered the pad I was using with my arms and slid it away from him. "Nothing," I said, my heart pounding like crazy. How had I not thought to cover it up first thing?

"You're making a list," Connor teased, grabbing for the pad. "Come on! What's it for?"

I knew he was just playing, but there was no way I could let him see what was on that paper. If I did my whole cover would be blown.

"It's Biff's and it's personal," I snapped, shoving the pad toward her.

She took it and slid it right into her lap. Connor's face fell, and I felt a lump rise up in my throat.

"Okay. Sorry," he said, looking nervous. "Are you mad at me about something?"

God. This was not going well. All I wanted to do was get the heck out of there. I was not good with confrontation. Especially when I was having a hard time figuring out my feelings and whether or not they were valid.

"Excuse me, Miss Morris?" ·

I looked up to find the doorman from my first day at the lodge hovering over the table, his hands behind his back. He was dressed in a suit today, which meant he was working the concierge desk instead of the front door.

"Hi," I said tentatively.

"Sorry to interrupt, but your mother wanted me to let you know that she's waiting for you in the salon."

Oh. Dear. God. My hair trial. Right. All the attendants had an appointment to practice styles for the wedding. I had completely spaced. I could have blamed Maid of Honor Biff for not reminding me, but she didn't even have to go, since she had next to no hair to play with.

"Your mother?" Connor asked.

Biff stared at me, dumbstruck. My brain immediately flipped into panic mode. I was so, so snagged.

"My . . . my mother isn't even here," I improvised, knowing even as I said it that there was no way it could work. The doorman knew my mother. They'd met. He'd seen her nearly choke me with her fur coat. "She's in New Jersey."

I glanced at my brothers. They were so engrossed in their game they didn't even know what I was saying. Thank goodness.

"Um, no. She's in the salon. With all the other bridesmaids?" the doorman said. Poor guy must have been so baffled.

"You've got it all wrong, man," Connor said with a laugh. "She's not a bridesmaid. She's the nanny." The guy's brow knit. He looked at the boys, at me, at Biff. I tried to send him a telepathic message to just walk away. One more word from him and there was no way I could get out of explaining. His eyes locked on mine and I silently begged.

"Oh. All right, then. I guess I was mistaken," he said finally. "Again, sorry to interrupt."

The doorman gave me a slight bow and then turned and walked away. I was so relieved I felt my insides deflate like a slow-leaking balloon. My nanny cover was still in tact—for the moment. But I had no idea how much longer I could keep this up. There were just too many lies circulating and too many people involved. Sooner or later, my worlds were going to collide and I was going to be screwed.

"Imagine, him thinking you were one of those girls." Connor smirked, his eyes teasing.

Something snapped inside my mind and heart and suddenly all the humiliations and insecurities I'd ever felt rushed forward. Maybe it was because I was already raw from the past couple of days and from my near unmasking, but his joke hit me hard. One look at me and he knew instantly that he'd said something wrong.

"What's that supposed to mean?" I asked, standing.

"Nothing!" he said, raising his hands. "I just . . . It's just you're not like one of those girls, you know, *those* girls."

"What? The girls who care about their appearance? The girls who know how to use a straightening iron?" I demanded. "The girls who are actual *girls*?"

Biff looked away as Connor stammered for a reply. "Jane, I—"

"Forget it," I said. "Boys, we're going."

"No! I wanna finish the game!" Ben whined.

"You two get up right now and I'll let you have banana splits for lunch," I said.

They were out of their chairs like they'd been ejected. For some reason, that small victory gave me a rush. I suppose I would have taken anything at that point.

"See you later, Biff," I said.

Then, without another word to Connor, the three of us walked out of there as fast as my brothers' short legs would allow.

Chapter 12

That night I awoke with a start when a knock landed on my door. It was pitch-black in my room, and the digital clock at my bedside read 1:05 A.M. I groaned, pushing myself up, as the light knocking repeated itself.

"This had better be some kind of huge hotel emergency," I grumbled as I tromped across the room. "Fire. Avalanche. Something."

I glanced through the peephole and almost died. Connor stood outside my door with a big bouquet of flowers and a hopeful expression. I looked down at my pajamas—an oversize New York Giants T-shirt and plaid flannel pants—and basically wanted to kill myself. *Why not just reaffirm his opinion of you, Farrah?* I looked around the room hopelessly. It wasn't like I could execute a quick change into a fashion plate. There wasn't one Victoria's Secret item in my possession. Instead I grabbed the hotel-issue white robe and yanked it on to cover most of my outfit. Then I took a deep breath, shook my hair back, and opened the door.

"I'm a jackass," he said.

I blinked. "Good opener."

He smiled slightly. "Did I wake you up?"

"Sort of," I said, not willing to let him off the hook just yet.

"Sorry. I just got off work and I had to talk to you. I knew that if I went home I'd drive myself crazy all night," he told me. "I'm really sorry about this morning. For what I said."

I stared at him, not sure what to say. I crossed my arms over my chest and leaned against the doorjamb, letting the heavy door rest on my butt. "Go on."

"Okay, well, I have a sister, Laura? She's in high school. So, well, I ran by her exactly what I said to you and, well, she hung up on me."

I smirked and he seemed buoyed by that.

"But then she called me back and she said I had insulted your female-hood and I was a misogynistic moron," he continued. "I didn't even think she knew the word *misogynistic*, but she does. Anyway. Did I insult your female-hood?" he asked, his eyebrows adorably raised.

"You could say that," I replied. I had to meet this sister of his. She was a smart girl.

"Well, then, I'm really sorry. But you should know I didn't mean to do that," Connor told me. "I don't think you don't care about your appearance. And I don't think that you don't know how to use that stuff you mentioned. I just figured you don't need any of it. Because, you know . . . well . . . look at you."

I blushed and my eyes hit the floor. "Please."

"No. I'm totally serious, Jane," Connor said, stepping forward. "You are *so* beautiful."

I must have been purple at that point. I stared at the laces on his shoes. He'd called me beautiful. Hot Connor Davy thought I was beautiful.

"Could you look at me, please?" he said, shifting his weight from foot to foot.

Somehow, I pulled my gaze off the floor and looked into his eyes. They were mere inches away. The only thing separating us was that big bouquet of flowers.

"I'm sorry if I made you feel anything less than that," he told me. "But as far as I'm concerned, you put those bridesmaid girls to shame."

"Th-thanks," I managed to say.

He grinned. "So. Am I forgiven?"

He handed me the flowers and I smiled. The first flowers I'd ever been given. But still, even with all the romance and stunning compliments, I didn't feel exactly right. Normally I'd probably just let it go, but I was getting so sick of lying. All I wanted right then was to be perfectly honest.

"You are, for that," I said, my stomach twisting into uncomfortable knots. "But there's something else."

"Gulp," Connor said aloud.

I laughed and toyed with a big pink petal on one of the flowers. "It's just, the stuff you said in that girl Carina's room. You were picking on all those things and it's just . . . you don't know why she has all that stuff. Why she might need it. I mean, maybe she feels badly about herself. You'd sort of have to feel badly about yourself to change yourself that much. To put in that much work. Wouldn't you?"

When I looked up at Connor again, he looked ill.

"I never really thought of it that way," he said.

"Well, I just felt really awful after we did that," I said.

He reached out and took my hand. "I'm really sorry," he said. "I was just messing around."

I smiled. "I know." I blew out a breath I hadn't realized I was holding. "Phew. It's hard, this honesty stuff."

He laughed and leaned forward to kiss my

forehead and I felt even more relief rush through my body. "There's something I want to show you, if you'll come."

"What is it?" I asked, intrigued.

"It's a surprise," he said.

Now that we'd talked I felt infinitely lighter. And perhaps up for a middle-of-the-night resort adventure. "Okay. Let me just get my key."

"Actually, you might want to put on that outfit," he said. "The one I made you change out of the other day? I felt bad that you never got to wear it."

Now I was *really* intrigued. "Okay," I said, giddy. "Give me ten minutes."

"I'll wait."

He took a step back and leaned against the far wall. The last thing I saw before I closed the door was his mischievous smile.

I was having déjà vu. Just like that first day in the hotel, I found myself sneaking through the hallway outside the ballroom in the middle of the night. But this time, I wasn't with crazy Biff, I was with Hot Connor. And this time, instead of being all frumped out in baggy jeans and an even baggier sweater, I was wearing my new skirt, my green top, and my cushy black flats. I had applied about ten coats of underarm deodorant and put my hair back in a ponytail so that it wouldn't have that wild, slept-on look, and I actually felt beautiful. Possibly because Connor kept looking at me with that spark in his eyes—like I was the only girl in the world.

"Where are we going?" I whispered, clutching his hand on our way down the hall.

"We're here," he said.

He stopped right outside the double doors to the ballroom. Connor grinned in self-satisfaction. I hugged myself against a sudden chill—one drawback of dressing girly was that it meant less insulation—and glanced around.

"We're where?" I asked.

"Jane Morris, welcome to paradise," Connor said.

He opened the door to the ballroom and warm, vanilla-scented air whooshed out at me, inviting me in. I stepped over the threshold and the sight before me took my breath away. All the tables save for one had been moved against the walls, and they were blanketed with black tablecloths and hundreds upon hundreds of white candles, flickering softly—the only light in the room. The table in the center of the space was set with two silver-domed trays and a low vase full of rosebuds sat in the center. Romantic guitar music played at a soothing volume over hidden speakers.

"Wow," I said under my breath.

"Well, maybe it's not paradise, exactly, but it was the best I could do on short notice," Connor said, stepping up next to me.

"No, Connor. It's . . . it's incredible," I told him.

My heart was full. I couldn't have daydreamed up a better surprise. This was exactly the kind of perfect moment I had always envisioned but could never really imagine happening in real life. This was a real romantic gesture. And it was all for me.

"Care to dance?" Connor asked, holding out his hand.

The first response that popped into my mind was *I can't dance.* My first instinct was to laugh and joke self-deprecatingly and back away. But I bit my tongue and somehow held my ground. There was only so much Connor could do to make this night perfect, and he'd already done it all. It was time for me to meet him halfway. If I wanted people to see my feminine side, I had to get used to showing it.

"Sure," I said. "I'd . . . love to."

He smiled and took my hand. Together we walked over to the center of the empty dance floor.

Just go with it, I told myself. *Try to let him lead or whatever. Just breathe.*

Connor paused and put his arms around my

hips, middle-school-dance style. For a moment, I hesitated, then I placed my arms on his shoulders and laughed.

"Sorry, this is all I got," Connor said, chagrined. "I'm not exactly *Dancing with the Stars* material."

"No, it's okay," I told him. "It's perfect, actually."

"We'll see if you're saying that in a few minutes when your toes are all bruised," Connor joked.

"I can handle it," I joked back.

Together we started to sway to the music, moving our feet only as much as we absolutely had to. Whenever my eye caught his I found myself blushing uncontrollably. But soon I got used to being so close to him, to feeling his breath on my cheek, and I was able to concentrate on other things. Like how warm I felt in his arms. How every time he moved his hands even just a touch, I felt a rush of attraction. How we seemed to be inching closer to each other with each passing moment.

"I want to say something, but it might come out all wrong," Connor said.

His voice sounded all husky and deep and it sent pleasant warm thrills all through me. There was absolutely nothing he could say right then that would sound wrong.

"What is it?" I asked.

"I just wanted you to know that it doesn't matter to me what you wear or don't wear or . . . or . . . whether you want to wear false eyelashes or makeup or shave your head or whatever," he said, his words tumbling into one another. He stopped moving and looked into my eyes. My heart flipped over and pounded hard. "No matter what you want to do . . . you're all girl to me, Jane."

Tears rushed to my eyes. There was nothing I could do to stop them. It was like every insecurity I'd ever felt had just burst at once. One single tear spilled over and raced down my cheek. Connor lifted his hand and touched the wet streak with his thumb.

"Did I say something wrong?" he asked.

"No," I said, smiling through the blur. "You just said something ridiculously right."

And then he smiled. And kissed me. And we went on to have the single most perfect date I could have ever wished for.

Chapter 13

"So, are you going to tell me about this guy or what?" Jonah asked. "I mean, you may as well tell me now, because you know I'm going to break you eventually. This way we can avoid the torture."

"Jonah . . ."

"Seriously. Just tell me. Was that the Connor kid you were telling me about the other day or have you already moved on to someone else?" Jonah asked me. "Farrah, have you become . . ." He put in a comical gasp. "A player?"

I laughed at the total ridiculousness of that idea.

"Look, I don't even know what you're talking about," I said, blushing. "I was not getting cozy with some guy on the porch on Christmas night."

Jonah was clearly amused. "Yeah, that's what Marni said you said."

"Well, you should listen to her. She is, after all,

going to be your wife," I told him.

We were walking through the lobby the next morning, headed for the café, which, as we now knew, served the best coffee and muffins of any restaurant at the resort. The sun was shining and it looked to be yet another perfect day. If I could just get Jonah off my case already.

"Excuse me, but I'm not insane," Jonah said, pausing in the warm sunlight pouring through one of the skylights. "I saw the dude with my own eyes. We both did. Tall. Blond. Way too pretty." I couldn't help grinning and Jonah's eyes lit up. "See? You can't tell me there was no guy! I mean, look at you. You even *look* different."

"Yeah. It's called new clothes," I said flatly.

I was wearing my nicest jeans and my new, ridiculously soft white sweater and feeling light as air. And maybe even a little bit pretty. It was amazing what some new clothes and a romantic few hours in the middle of the night with an incredible guy could do. I think I was even standing up straighter.

"No. It's not just that. You're, like, glowing," Jonah said. I rolled my eyes and kept walking, and Jonah, of course, followed. "I don't understand why you won't tell me. I'm supposed to be your brother over here."

His voice grew slightly serious and I felt a pang of guilt. But I knew that if I told my brother that my crush worked here at the hotel, he'd want to meet him, and that could not happen without blowing my nanny cover. Things were going too well with Connor right now. I wasn't going to risk screwing them up. Honestly, I wouldn't even be walking around with my brother in public if I didn't know that Connor had the morning off.

"Jonah, I—"

I stopped talking as we stepped into the reception area and a bevy of loud, raucous voices surrounded us, bouncing off the vaulted ceiling and echoing to every corner. Jonah and I looked at each other and immediately we both forgot what we had been talking about.

"Uh-oh," I said.

A wide smile slowly spread across Jonah's face. "They're he-ere!" he sang.

"Yeah. But *where*?" I asked, looking around.

At that moment David Gelb, Nicholas Johnson, and Seth Schwartz came loping around the huge Christmas tree garden that had been planted in the fountain at the center of the lobby. Short-but-ripped David wore a Santa hat and dragged a huge suitcase behind him, tall and gangly Nicholas had an inflatable naked woman under his arm, and

Seth, as usual, brought up the rear, rolling his eyes at his friends' antics.

"Buttheads!" Jonah shouted happily.

"Jon-ass! And Little Red!" Nicholas replied, his eyes lighting up. He dropped everything, including the inflatable girl, and rushed forward. After slapping hands with my brother, he went to grab me into a hug, but instead twisted me under his arm and hit me with a first-class noogie.

"Ow!" I shouted, wincing. "Have you been sharpening your knuckles?"

"Wuss," he said, releasing me.

I stood up and slapped hands with David, who then pulled me toward him for a quick squeeze. My heart fluttered and I had to laugh at myself.

"Little Red, you look outstanding," he said when I stepped back. "You're, like, hot."

"Dude. That's my sister," Jonah said.

"Just stating the obvious, friend," David replied.

I snorted a laugh and felt a hot blush creep up my face. I'd harbored a fairly intense crush on David most of my life, one that had only been slightly tempered when I'd sprouted in the eighth grade and started looming half a foot above his head, even though he had three years on me. Basically, this compliment was like a dream come true. I had always thought I was invisible to my brother's friends—except as a person to pick on, order around, or play video games with. The idea of David seeing me as a hot girl was totally new.

"Um, thanks," I said, biting my lip as my brother hugged his friends. "Hi, Seth. How was your flight?"

"Hey, Farrah. Bumpy. Thanks for asking," he replied, fishing in his bag for something.

"So, what took you guys so long?" I asked. "We've been here forever already."

"We know, we know. It must have been very dull around this place without us," David lamented with a nod. "I mean, look at it. What a dump!" he joked. Then he shoved my brother, who shoved him back, and before I knew it they were practically wrestling at my feet. Nicholas watched with glee while Seth ignored them.

"Jonah wanted us to come out last week, but some of us actually have to work for a living," Seth told me. He'd finally found his PDA and was now checking the screen, even as the words were escaping his lips.

"Would you lighten up already, Schwartz?!" Nicholas cried, pulling Seth into his side, hard. "We're here now. It's vacation! Unplug already."

He grabbed the PDA out of Seth's hand and

held it away from him.

"Oh. That's very mature," Seth said. "Give it back."

"Come and get it!" Nicholas taunted, holding it high over his head. Which, by the way, was so high even Kobe Bryant would have had trouble jumping for it, let alone Seth Schwartz, who had been blessed with sprinter's speed but absolutely no vertical leap. While I was standing there, watching these four college graduates act like kindergartners, Biff materialized beside me.

"So, what's this? WWE tryouts?" she asked.

"Nope. Just Jonah's friends," I replied happily.

David extricated himself from my brother's choke hold and stood up.

"David Gelb, at your service," he said, offering his hand. "Ignore those dorks." He pointed over his shoulder with his thumb at Nicholas, Seth, and Jonah. My brother had joined in the fun and was helping Nick torture Seth. "They're still drunk from the plane."

"But it's nine A.M." Biff said.

"Yes, but the booze was free," David deadpanned.

"Touché," Biff responded, clearly impressed. "I'm Biff, by the way."

"Pleasure to meet a girl with such interesting

hair," David said, eyeing her platinum head.

"Happy to know a grown man who walks around in a Santa hat," Biff countered.

David grinned. "I like her," he told me.

"She's a keeper," I agreed.

Behind David, Seth climbed up on a chair and made a grab for the PDA and ended up sprawled flat on his face, which sent both Jonah and Nicholas into fits of laughter. Nick doubled over, leaving the PDA unprotected for the moment. Seth reached up from the floor, snatched it, and ran. The second Nicholas realized this, the race was on. All three of them sprinted out of there, leaving their luggage and their naked lady behind them.

"Excuse me," Biff said gleefully. "I gotta see how this one ends." Then she took off after the other guys, nearly knocking over an old woman who was traversing the lobby with her mini poodle.

"Ah. It's so good to see you guys," I said with a nostalgic sigh.

"Of course it is," David replied.

"I was just going to get some coffee. Wanna come?" I asked.

"Is the Pope Polish? Oh, wait. He's not anymore, is he?"

I laughed and we started to walk toward the café, David's monster suitcase bumping along on its wheels behind us. I glanced over my shoulder and saw one of the bellboys loading Nicholas's and Seth's stuff onto a cart. They really were efficient around this place.

"So, Little Red, let's talk bachelor party," David said, reaching his arm around my back. I smiled to myself at the gesture. A couple of years ago, that mere touch would have sent me into ecstatic giggles. But now, it was just kind of nice. Guess I was officially a Connor-centered being. "We only have, like, a day, so we're going to have to get right to work."

"Uh, don't worry. I've already got it covered," I replied.

"Yeah. Sure you do," David said as we stepped up to the counter.

"No. I actually do," I told him. "They have this great party planner here who's been really helpful. I think it's going to be really fun."

"Um, no offense, Little Red, but you're a girl," David said.

I pressed my lips together to keep from grinning. People had been noticing that fact a lot lately. I ordered a couple of coffees and muffins for me and for Jonah when he returned, then let David order.

"So because I'm a girl I can't plan a bachelor

party?" I asked, leaning against the counter as we waited for our food.

"Categorically impossible," David said firmly.

"Well, I think you're going to be pleasantly surprised," I told him.

David narrowed his eyes at me. "We'll see, Little Red. We'll see."

I stood in front of the mirror in my bathroom, stunned into speechlessness at my reflection. For the first time since it had arrived at the student post office, I was wearing my best man's dress. I had been dreading this moment for weeks, knowing that my boobs wouldn't fill it out, that my shoulders would look huge, that the fabric would be itchy and I'd be uncomfortable and I'd feel like a fraud. But now, staring at myself from every possible angle I could think of, there was one thing I had to admit: I looked *good*.

A giddy grin broke out across my face just as Biff rapped impatiently on the door. "You're gonna have to come out of there sooner or later!"

I took a deep breath and turned toward the door. The skirt swished around my ankles and the netty part underneath tickled my skin. I tried not to laugh, and opened the door.

Biff's eyes widened as she slowly looked me up

and down. "Oh my God. I hate my sister."

My stomach and heart dropped together as one. "What? Why?"

Biff turned around and tromped back toward the main area of my room. I followed, my hands pressed against the bodice of my dress. She sat down on one of the beds and flopped backward, flinging her arm over her eyes.

"Oh God. What? Does it look that bad?" I asked. Man, I really was clueless about this fashion stuff. I had thought I looked pretty darn good. And sophisticated. And maybe even a tiny bit sexy.

"No! It looks *insanely* good!" Biff cried, sitting up again. "It's so much cooler than the bag she's making me wear!"

I laughed and slapped my hand over my mouth. "Really?"

I turned to check myself out in the full-length mirror near the closet now, feeling almost like I was playing dress-up for Halloween. Although all my Halloween costumes had been very different than this—ninjas and football players and super-heroes. But one thing was for certain: I had been transformed. The tight bodice totally accented my slim waist and the wide, low neckline minimized my shoulders while actually creating cleavage. It was as if the dress was made for me. I guess that was why Marni was in fashion design. She knew exactly what to get to play up the good parts of my body and play down the bad.

"Marni has pretty good taste, huh?" I said finally.

"Annoyingly, yeah," Biff grumbled.

I was startled by a sudden knock at the door. My mother was supposed to be stopping by to check out the dress and I had a feeling she was going to freak when she saw me—in a good way. I was about to just fling open the door, when our visitor spoke.

"Special room service delivery for Jane Morris!"

The blood froze in my veins and I stopped with my hand on the doorknob.

"It's Connor!" I hissed, whirling to face Biff. The dress made a swooshing sound so loud I hoped he couldn't hear it.

"Omigod! He cannot see you in that dress. Take it off!" she whispered.

I groped for the zipper at my back but found my hands were suddenly sweaty. "Help me!" I whispered, panicked.

Biff jumped up and unzipped the dress in one quick motion. I wrestled my arms out of the arm-holes and let the pouf of fabric fall to my ankles, then tripped myself trying to step out of it.

"Jane? You in there?"

"Uh, yeah!" I cried, standing in the middle of my room half naked now.

Biff grabbed up the dress and shoved it in the closet, then threw me my sweater.

"Just a second!" I shouted.

"She's not decent!" Biff added.

"Really? Then I'm coming in!" Connor joked. He played with the doorknob and I screamed. I knew that he had a master key to the place attached to his belt.

"No! Do not open that door!" I wailed, crossing my arms over my chest.

"Don't worry. I was just kidding."

"Oh. Ha-ha," I shot back.

I rolled my eyes as I struggled into my jeans. Amazing how difficult something like dressing myself became when I was in a nervous rush. I untwisted my sweater, which was all clumped up under my arm, and headed for the door, just as Biff closed the closet. We looked at each other and both took a breath. Everything was fine. Nothing suspicious lying around. Good. I let Connor in.

"Hi!" I said with a bright smile as he pushed a room service cart into the room.

"Hey. What were you guys doing in here?" He looked around as if hoping for clues.

"Nothing. Just trying on clothes," Biff said. "You know us girls."

Connor looked at her for a second, disturbed. Not that I could blame him. She sounded like she was on speed or something.

"Well, I brought you guys a little something from downstairs," he said, removing the dome on the food tray with a flourish. Sitting there on a round platter was an entire chocolate layer cake.

"Oh my God! I *love* you!" Biff cried.

Connor laughed. "The bakery somehow got the order wrong and made half a dozen more than we need. So go crazy."

"Don't have to ask me twice," Biff said, unwrapping a fork from its linen napkin.

"Jane, could I talk to you over here for a sec?" Connor asked.

"Uh, sure."

He took my hand and led me back toward the door for privacy. My heart thumped loudly in my chest, both from the near miss of him finding me in my ball gown and from a new nervousness. What, exactly, did he want to talk to me about?

"So, listen," he said, lacing his fingers through mine and holding our hands up. "I was wondering . . . do you want to hang out on New Year's Eve?"

I immediately felt a thrill of unadulterated excitement. A date for New Year's Eve? That was something I'd never had before. We could drink champagne and kiss at midnight and . . .

Suddenly all my insides hollowed out. New Year's Eve? Oh, God. This was so not good. How had I not seen this coming? Of course he wanted to hang out on New Year's Eve. It was one of the most couple-y nights of the year. But little did he know I had a previous engagement that night. Namely, watching my brother get married.

"Jane?" he prompted.

"Oh, sorry. I . . . It's just, I . . ." I wracked my brain for a response. What could Jane the nanny possibly be doing on New Year's Eve? Oh, right! Duh. "I have to watch the boys, you know, while the Janssens are at the wedding."

Phew. God. How perfect was that?

"Oh, well, I figured," he said. "I was kind of talking about after midnight anyway. When the wedding's over."

"You were?" I asked.

"Yeah. I mean, I have to work this monster shindig and everything, so I won't even be free until like two A.M., but I thought if you could stay up . . ."

He made this incredibly cute, provocative face

and toyed with my hands, but I barely even noticed. The room was whirling and the last week and a half was flashing before my eyes. I closed my eyes for a moment, feeling for certain that I was about to throw up.

Connor was working the wedding. He was going to be at the wedding. The wedding that he thought I had no part in. He was going to see me in my gown. He was going to watch me take pictures with the groom. He might even be present for the all-important speech I had yet to write.

The jig, as they say, was up.

"So? What do you say?" he asked. "We could even count down to a fake midnight and do the whole first-kiss-of-the-new-year thing. Wanna spend the first morning of the new year with me?"

Somehow, in all the vertigo, I managed to find my voice. "So much," I said.

Connor grinned. "Good. I will call you the *second* I'm released from wedding hell."

I swallowed hard and nodded. "Sounds good."

"Good," Connor said. Then he leaned in and kissed me quickly on the lips. "Enjoy the cake!" he called over to Biff.

"I am!" she said, her words muffled by her full mouth.

Connor laughed, gave me one last smile, and

then walked out. I stepped back into the bedroom area, keeping my shoulder pressed to the wall so that I wouldn't fall over. Biff was gulping at a glass of milk when I arrived, but she quickly lowered it when she saw my face.

"What? He didn't break up with you, did he? That bastard. Plying you with chocolate before he—"

"He didn't break up with me," I said. "He's going to be working the wedding."

Biff's fork hit the plate with a clatter. "No."

"Yeah."

There was a long moment of silence as the gravity of this fact ever so slowly sunk in.

"What am I going to do, Biff?" I asked finally.

Biff, for once, stared back at me with a blank expression. "I have absolutely no idea."

"So? What do you think?" Emily asked me the following morning.

What am I going to do? What am I going to do???

"Farrah? Are you okay?"

She touched my arm and I finally snapped to.

"What?" I blurted.

"I asked you if you like it. Is it what you were envisioning?" she asked. "Is there anything you'd like to add or change? Because we still have plenty of time before the party tonight."

For the first time I forced myself to take a good, long look around the room. Instead of taking one of the ballrooms for the bachelor party, Emily had secured the Presidential Suite in the penthouse of the hotel. There was a tremendous, modern living room with a full bar in one corner and three huge, cushy couches set up to face three even more monster televisions, which workmen were now installing. Emily had also brought in vintage pin-ball machines and arcade games, a dart board, and a couple of Skee-Ball games. The walls were deco-rated with posters and ads for everything from Asteroids to Super Mario Brothers, from Tomb Raider to Doom. It was all totally immature and absolutely, ridiculously cool. Unfortunately, I couldn't get psyched about it because I still felt like someone had punched me in the stomach. I'd felt that way ever since Connor's New Year's Eve invite. Still, Emily was looking at me expectantly, so I had to say something.

"It's absolutely perfect," I told her. "Jonah is going to love it."

"I'm so glad," she said with a smile. "And there are two bedrooms attached to the suite, so if anyone gets too . . . out of control, they can just sleep it off here instead of having to find their way back to their own rooms."

"That's great," I replied, trying to sound enthused.

"Is something wrong? Like I said, we can still make changes if you want." She produced her clipboard and had a pen at the ready.

Okay, it was time for me to start acting like a grown-up here, and focus. My problems were not Emily's problems. I turned and looked her directly in the eye.

"Nothing's wrong. You did an incredible job," I assured her.

"*We* did," she amended, and I laughed.

"Okay, *we* did."

The door behind us opened and Biff stepped into the room, closing the door quickly behind her. She was wearing black-and-white-striped stockings and some kind of denim jumper thing. Emily tensed. I can only imagine that, to her, Biff looked like some vagabond off the street.

"Hey! There you are. I've been looking all over for you!" Biff said urgently.

My heart took a nosedive. What had happened now?

"Can I help you?" Emily asked, stepping in front of me like she was my bodyguard or something.

"Uh, no. Can I help *you*?" Biff said.

"Emily, this is Biff . . . Buffy, uh, Shay," I said. "Marni's sister?"

Emily blanched and placed her hand to her chest. "Oh. I'm so sorry. I didn't recognize you. Of course."

"Happens all the time," Biff said flatly. "Now could I talk to my friend, please?"

"Of course. I'll just go check on the bar," Emily said. "It's been a pleasure working with you, Farrah."

She offered her hand and I shook it. "You, too. Thanks, Emily," I replied, hoping she wouldn't notice the cold sweat that had suddenly popped up on my palm. If she did, she didn't mention it, and soon Biff and I were alone.

"What's going on? Did something happen?" I asked Biff. "Oh, God. Did my brother and Marni track down Connor?"

"No. No. Nothing's wrong," Biff told me. She led me over to the nearest couch and plopped down, tucking her foot up underneath her. "It's just, I think I know what you have to do to fix the situation."

"You do?" I said hopefully.

"Yeah, but I don't know if you're going to go for it."

Already the hope was dashed. What could she possibly have in mind anyway? She couldn't have come up with anything I hadn't landed on during my full night of tossing and turning.

"Fake the flu, right? Go down for the count," I said, sitting next to her. I had come up with that one somewhere around three A.M. and at the time, it had seemed like the only viable option. Although now it sounded insane. Like my mother would ever let me get away with missing my brother's wedding. I'd have to be dead first.

"No," Biff said seriously. "I think you have to come clean."

"What?" I blurted. "You've got to be kidding."

"Look, you're going to have to do it eventually, anyway," Biff told me. "Think about it. What if you and Connor go back to school and start dating seriously? Sooner or later he's going to want to meet your family. Or even if he doesn't, he's going to be in your room and he's going to see a picture of you and Jonah. Then you'll have some serious explaining to do."

I slumped down against the soft cushions. I'd never thought that far ahead before, but she did have a point. Did I really expect Connor to think I was a nanny forever?

"At least if you tell him the truth now you can

get through tomorrow without playing hide-and-seek all day," Biff said. "Which, while it could be slapstick hilarious, is kind of impractical."

I took a deep breath and let it out slowly. She was right. Of course she was right. But why did I suddenly feel so indescribably heavy? Why did my eyes suddenly sting with a vengeance?

"He's going to hate me," I said quietly.

"I don't think so," Biff said. "That's just it. Connor's a cool guy. I think that if you explain it right, he's going to understand."

A few feet away, a couple of the worker guys fired up one of the TVs and started testing out a boxing game. The volume was up so loud it felt as if the punching sound effects were reverberating in my bones. *Left jab! Uppercut! Oh, a right hook to the gut!* the digital announcer shouted.

"But what if I don't explain it right?" I said to Biff.

"You will," Biff said firmly.

On the screen, one of the guys slammed a fist into the other guy's head and the head flew off, spurting blood everywhere. *"Oh! KO'd!"* the announcer shouted mirthfully. *"That's gonna leave a stain."*

"I will?"

Biff sighed grimly. "You're gonna have to."

Chapter 14

"All right, Little Red, I take it back. This party is sick!" David shouted, slapping me on the shoulder. He had to shout to be heard over the loud music and the cacophony of three different video games blasting from three different huge TVs. He hoisted himself up onto the suede bar stool next to mine and spun around to face the room.

"Not too shabby, huh?" I asked, taking a sip of my soda.

"Not too shabby," he confirmed. "Even if there are no strippers," he added with a wink. He finished off his beer and dropped the mug on top of the bar, then glanced at me tentatively. "Are there really no strippers?"

"Yeah. There are really no strippers. But what about the sexy waitresses? I did get the sexy waitresses," I pointed out.

Just then Tashana, a tall, gorgeous woman in fishnets and a minidress, strolled by with a platter full of grilled cheese sandwiches. She grinned at David and leaned toward him with the platter, showing off some seriously ample cleavage.

"Grilled cheese?" she asked, lifting her perfect eyebrows.

David snorted. "You could be serving up liver and onions and I'd take it."

He snatched a couple of sandwiches and tore into one, checking out her butt as she strolled away. I shook my head at him and turned my attention to the big screen in the center of the room as a loud cheer went up for Jonah. He threw his arms in the air and stood up, still clutching his controller.

"That's what I'm *talkin'* about!" he shouted, taunting Nicholas, who hung his head on the couch. His inflatable girl was sitting next to him like a supportive date. "Winner and *still* champion! I think that deserves another round of beer!"

All his friends cheered and the waitresses jumped to, bringing over frothing mugs and providing new trays of pizza. I laughed as Jonah shoved half a slice into his mouth.

"Farrah, this has to be the best bachelor party on record," he said, coming over to hug me. He reeked of beer and was already getting a little rubbery in the limbs, but that was what this night was supposed to be about, right? His last night to get crazy. "Where did you get these TVs? And the waitresses? We really like the waitresses."

"The waitresses were actually Biff's idea," I told him, patting him on the back as he draped his arm over my shoulder. "She said that if I wasn't going to get strippers I had to provide some kind of eye candy."

"Well, it is *sweet*," Jonah said with a nod. "Not that it matters. The only candy I want from here on out is Marni's candy. That candy is *all* mine."

"Okay. This conversation just took a disturbing turn for me," I told him.

His eyes widened and he covered his mouth. "Oh! Sorry. Sometimes I forget, you know? That you're not just one of the guys."

"Dude. I told you. Your sister's hot!" David said. "She could not be one of the guys."

Jonah's eyes grew serious. "Don't make me hit you, man."

I laughed and David threw his hands up in surrender. "I'm gonna go play Madden. You two bond or . . . whatever."

David made his way over to the TV on the far side of the room and joined a couple of Jonah's college friends on the couch. Everyone was laughing and eating and drinking and cheering, and they had been ever since the party started a few hours earlier. Even Mr. Shay had stuck around for more than an hour, playing darts with Jonah and the other guys from the wedding party. He had thanked me for an enjoyable and surprisingly original evening before he left. I was sure he appreciated the non-stripper decision.

"We *should* bond," Jonah said, leaning back against the bar. "Is there something you want to play?"

"Nah. You should hang out with your friends," I told him. "This is a guy's night."

"But you're my best friend. I want to hang out with you," Jonah told me.

I would be lying if I said that comment didn't touch me to my very core. I suddenly felt nostalgic for every single moment my brother and I had ever spent together. He was right. If this was his last night as a single guy—the last night of his old life— then I should be a big part of it.

"Okay, fine," I said, jumping off my stool. "How about I school you in Skee-Ball?"

"Shyeah. Like that's gonna happen," Jonah said, hooking his arm around my neck as we made our way toward the games. "I *own* you at Skee-Ball."

"You wish!"

"*You* wish!"

I looked at him, my brow knitting. "That doesn't even make any sense."

Jonah stared at me for a long moment, then laughed. "You're right! You know, I think I may be a little drunk."

I cracked up and patted him on the back. "Yeah. This is going to be the easiest win of my life."

"I really love Marni, you know?" Jonah said, leaning most of his weight into my side as the elevator descended. He had a pizza sauce stain on the front of his light blue sweater and, for some reason, one of his pants legs was rolled up practically to his knee. "I, like, love her *so* much."

"Yes. I know," I told him. One arm was around his waist, holding him up, while the other hand clutched his sport jacket and his goody bag, which was filled with all the newest video games. Biff had been right about that one, too. All the guys had gone bonkers when they'd seen their parting gifts.

Jonah lifted his head like it weighed four thousand pounds and looked at me with his eyes at half-mast. "You do?"

"Oh, God!" I held my breath and winced. He smelled like onions and beer and some other sour smell I could not identify. "What did you *eat* tonight?"

"Everything. I ate everything," Jonah said, then burped. At least this time he covered his mouth. "There was a lot of good food. You know, you should be a party planner when you grow up."

"Yeah. My dream come true," I told him. "I'll get on that right after I become the first female booth analyst at the Super Bowl."

"Okay. Sounds like a plan," Jonah said with a serious nod. The elevator pinged and he gasped. "We're here!"

I had to laugh at that one. "Yes. We're here. Now, do you think you can walk?"

"Surenoproblem," he said, all one word.

Together we stumbled out of the elevator and I steered my big brother in the direction of his room. He was a bit wobbly on his feet, but not too bad. I would have left him in one of the suite bedrooms, but a couple of his friends had been even worse off than he was, so I'd let them have the beds instead. At least I knew where Jonah's room was, so I was able to get him back to it. It might have taken me all night to deliver all those guys to their various rooms.

"Have *you* ever been in love?" Jonah asked me as we slowly wove our way down the hall.

Instantly a picture of Connor appeared in my mind's eye and my heart felt all light and warm. Was I *in love* with him? Nah. Not possible. We'd only just started dating. But I had been pretty seriously crushing on him for months now. Maybe I sort of loved him. Almost. Possibly.

"I don't know," I said finally.

"Oh, well, then you haven't. Cuz when you're in love, you know it. Trust me," Jonah said, patting me on the head.

"Okay then," I told him. I stopped in front of his room and fished his key card out of his jacket pocket.

"Hey! This is my room!" he announced loudly.

"Yep."

I opened the door and held it for him. He smiled down at me and slapped me twice on the cheek before passing me by. "You're a sweet kid."

I rolled my eyes. "Gee, thanks."

Since it was the middle of the night, I closed the door quietly before following him inside. Jonah sat down on one of the beds and went about trying to untie his shoes. He kept missing the lace, though, and looked mightily confused.

"How about you just slip them off?" I suggested, putting his stuff down on the table.

"Good idea."

But instead, he dropped back on the bed and lay there like a wet rag. I sighed and fell to my knees at his feet.

"A best man's work is never done," I said.

"I know you don't want me to get married," Jonah announced.

My heart fell, and I was glad that at the moment, he couldn't see my face. "I don't not want you to get married."

"Yes, you do. You think I'm too young," he told me. "You think Marni's too high-maintenance. But she's not, you know. She's actually really low-maintenance. She knows who she is and she knows what she wants and she knows how to make me happy. She doesn't need, like, any main-tenance. At all."

I smirked as I pulled off his shoes. I had never looked at the whole high-maintenance, low-maintenance thing that way. I always figured if the girl was wealthy and accustomed to a certain style of living, that made her HM. But I could see what Jonah was saying about Marni. She wasn't needy. She wasn't insecure. She had a great career and a lot of self-confidence. Of course all that would add up to LM.

"That's good, Jonah," I said sincerely.

"And I love her," he said, lifting his head.

"That's the most important thing. When you love someone, you don't mess with it. You've gotta make sure you do everything you can not to lose it. Because, you know, who knows what's gonna happen? You could just wake up one day and they're not there."

I stared at him, my eyes filling up. "Like Dad."

"Like Dad," he said with a nod.

I took a deep, shaky breath and stood up. "C'mere," I said, grabbing his wrists. I sat him up, then yanked off his stained sweater over his head. He managed to stay sitting long enough for me to pull the covers down and toss half the unneeded pillows off onto the floor.

"Okay. Lay down and get some sleep," I told him.

Jonah did as he was told, cuddling into the pillow I'd left him. I lifted the blankets up over his shoulders and smiled.

"Tomorrow I get married," he said with a smile.

"Yeah. Tomorrow," I said.

Then I leaned over and kissed the top of his head and he sighed. I went into the bathroom and brought back the garbage can to leave by his bed, just in case.

"Love you, Farrah," Jonah mumbled, already half asleep.

"Love you, Jonah," I replied.

Then I turned out the lights and walked out, closing the door quietly behind me.

Out in the hallway, I leaned back against the wall, overwhelmed. My heart felt like it might burst as thoughts of my father and my childhood and my brother and Marni flooded through me. All at once I felt sad for everything that was ending, but so happy and excited for my brother and the new life he was about to start. One that would hopefully be filled with all the love he had always missed growing up. The love we had both missed.

A tear spilled down my cheek and I wiped it away quickly and took a deep breath. Suddenly I knew more than ever that Biff was right. I had to come clean with Connor or risk losing him forever. And as of that second, that was a risk I was not willing to take.

New Year's Eve dawned bright and crisp. The perfect weather for a confession. A perfect day to start over. Even though I had spent half the night sitting at the desk by the window, working on my best-man speech, I was wide awake when my alarm went off. This was a big day, not just for Jonah, but for me as well. I threw on my Colorado University sweatshirt and a pair of jeans and headed out bright and early to track down Connor. Somehow, I actually felt excited. Nervous as all get-out, too, of course, but excited. Whatever happened, at least I could finally get all the secrets off my chest. And in the back of my mind were Biff's assurances that Connor would understand. She was so certain about that fact that it made me feel almost certain, too. I would tell him and he would be shocked, but he would soon be fine. I mean, it wasn't the biggest lie in the world. It wasn't like I was telling him I was an alien or I was married or something. I was just telling him that my family had some money and my brother was marrying the richest girl on the planet. Big whoop. It was going to be fine.

I speed-walked from the elevator and into the lobby. I needed to get this over with before all the festivities began, including the rehearsal breakfast, which would start in about an hour. My plan was to go to the concierge desk and ask them where Connor was working that morning, but I didn't even have to do that. When I walked into the sunlit great room, Connor was standing right in the center by the Christmas trees, going over something with another concierge.

My heart constricted at the sight of him. He was wearing a tuxedo—probably the required uniform for the point man on an event the size of the Shay wedding—and he looked incredibly gorgeous. I had trouble believing that a guy like that had ever kissed me, let alone that he would still like me after I completely blew his mind. But I squared my shoulders and kept moving. He was still Connor. Just red-carpet-worthy Connor. I was determined to get this over with no matter what he was wearing. There would be no comfort for me all day long if I didn't. As I approached, he and the girl he was working with finished their conversation and she walked away. Perfect timing. It was like a sign that I was doing the right thing.

"Good morning," I said, stepping up next to him.

His face lit up when he saw me. "Good morning right back. Excuse the penguin suit," he said, touching his lapels. "It's a job hazard."

"No. You look . . ." There were no words, and I didn't have time to think of one. "Do you . . . um . . . have a second?" I asked, glancing around. I felt a bit exposed, standing in the center of the bustling lobby. The wedding guests were everywhere at this point and someone was bound to recognize me.

"Sure, but only a second," he said. "This wedding's got me booked all day long."

"Right. The wedding. That's kind of what I

wanted to talk to you about." My hands shook and I felt as if my heart was expanding and trying to eat my stomach. I just had to get this out. Just get it out and everything would be fine. "Connor, about the wedding. I'm kind of—"

"Farrah! There you are!"

Suddenly a deep pit of blackness opened up beneath my feet. My mother came scurrying across the room toward me in a casual pantsuit, all made up and coiffed and perfumed to high heaven. Behind her, much to my aneurysm, were the McNabbs. Tommy McNabb's parents. Mr. McNabb's coat was folded over his arm and Mrs. McNabb still wore hers. They looked as if they'd just stepped off the plane.

"Oh, God," I said. This was it. My life was over. All I could do now was watch the train coming and wait for it to hit me in the face.

Connor looked at me, baffled, as my mother stepped right up to me and grabbed both my arms. I tried to communicate something to him with my eyes—anything—but what? *I'm so sorry for what you're about to hear*, was all I could muster. Of course he just stared back at me, confused.

"Farrah, I have the biggest surprise for you!" my mother said, oblivious to Connor's existence or to the fact that she'd just interrupted me in the middle of a conversation. "I finally found you a date for the wedding!"

Then, like a horror movie come to life, the McNabbs parted and revealed their son, Tommy "Devil-Spawn" McNabb himself, standing there in his trendy frat-boy sweater and pants with his patented smirk on his annoyingly handsome face. Still gorgeous, that boy. Still freakishly, painfully gorgeous. I hated him.

"Oh my God," was pretty much the only phrase present in my vocabulary.

"I know! Aren't you so excited? Tommy was kind enough to cancel his New Year's plans and fly out with his parents last minute," my mother said, clutching me in one arm now, her hip to my hip. "Well? Say hello, Farrah. Don't be rude. The boy did fly all the way out here so you wouldn't have to be alone at your own brother's wedding."

I glanced at Connor. He was as white as a sheet. He'd just heard everything he needed to hear to know exactly how much I'd been lying to him for the past week and a half. Everything that I had so badly wanted to tell him myself, but just didn't get the chance. And he'd heard all of it while watching my mother practically shove me into Devil-Spawn's arms.

"Farrah," my mother said through her teeth.

I somehow swallowed the massive toad that had taken up residence in my throat. "Hi, Tommy."

"Hey, Farrah." Tommy lifted his chin in acknowledgment. "Nice . . . sweatshirt."

I immediately felt about as attractive as a warthog. There was a mocking smile in his eyes so obvious that I wondered how no one else could see it. But they didn't. His parents and my mother just gazed at him reverently like he was some golden god descended from on high to bless them with his presence. I crossed my arms over my chest as hot tears of humiliation filled my eyes. How could my mother do this to me after I had expressly asked her not to? And *Tommy McNabb*, of all people. This was the singlemost horrifying moment of my life. And Connor was there to witness it all

"I'm sorry. Can I help you?" my mother said suddenly. She glared at Connor.

"Actually, I don't think you can," Connor said, staring right at me. "But maybe . . . *Farrah* could explain?"

I wanted to die. Seriously. I wanted something to fall from the ceiling and hit me on the head. I wanted the entire place to crumble under a sudden avalanche. Anything to make this moment end.

"I . . ."

"Farrah? Who *is* this person?" my mother

asked, still clutching me in her one-armed death grip.

I fought for control of my faculties. Tried to think of some way to come out of this with any sort of dignity. "It's . . . this is . . ."

I gave up. I couldn't explain it. I couldn't fix it. Standing there in front of Tommy and his parents I just lost the will to fight. I fell silent and stared at the floor.

"I'm no one, Mrs. Janssen," Connor said coolly. "I just work here."

Then he turned around and walked away.

Chapter 15

I was scum. I felt like scum. I looked like scum. I was the scummiest bridesmaid/best man ever to walk the face of the earth. I sat in front of the makeup mirror in the sun-drenched bridal suite as all the other bridesmaids flitted around, sipping champagne and touching up their gloss and oohing and ahhing over Marni. My hair had been twisted up into a stylish chignon and the world-renowned makeup artist/friend of the Shays' (who had been flown in from Paris by the family) had given me the perfect, subtly made-up face, yet I was still nothing but scum.

"Farrah! Go put on your gown!" my mother said, clutching both my shoulders from behind. She looked around as if she was worried that someone might be listening in. "As much as I know you want to wear your pajamas down the aisle, it's not going to happen," she hissed in my ear.

I glared at her in the mirror, trying with all my

might to incinerate her with my eyes. I was so livid that, for a moment, I actually thought it might work, but it didn't. What was wrong with me? How had I let myself believe that she and I had made some progress? So we'd gone shopping together and she had actually listened to what I thought about the clothes. So she'd given me something I wanted for Christmas. Because of those small victories I had thought she understood where I was coming from with the whole pity-date thing? Talk about dumb. Clearly I'd just been deluding myself. My mother wanted me to be the person she had always envisioned I'd be. Someone like Marni—all feminine and perfect and datable. The real me was invisible to her. Sooner or later I was going to have to get that through my thick head.

"What are you waiting for?" my mother asked, oblivious to my death glare. "Go!"

I shoved myself up and trudged over to the dressing room, where my gown was the last one hanging on the hooks, surrounded by bare hangers and garment bags. Empty shoe boxes were strewn all around the room along with big tote bags full of the other girls' hair products and curling irons and perfume and jewelry options. All I had was my one shoe box and my dress.

"You okay? Did you find Connor this morning?" Biff asked, slipping in at the last minute and closing the door behind her. At the rehearsal breakfast, there had never been a good time to tell her what had gone on between me and Connor, and I was somewhat relieved to see her now.

"You look great, Biff," I said morosely. "That is no bag."

The halter-style dress Marni had chosen for her maid of honor, with its slim straps and flowing style, looked fabulous on Biff. With her dark-rimmed eyes and pouty lips, she could have stepped right off the set of *America's Next Top Model*.

"Thanks for the enthusiasm," Biff joked when she heard my blah tone. "What happened? Did you tell him the truth?"

"No. My mother did," I said, my shoulders drooping.

"What?" Biff asked with a gasp.

"And let's just say he did not take it well," I told her. "Oh, and not only that, my mom also invited Tommy McNabb to be my date for the wedding."

"Omigod! No way. Evil incarnate is here?" She dropped into a chair like lead.

"And he wasn't even preceded by a rain of toads," I joked lamely.

"God, Farrah. How are you even standing right now?"

"I have to," I said with a shrug. I reached up and took down my dress, feeling nostalgic for the other day when I had fallen in love with it. Now I just wanted to ball it up and toss it in the trash and skip this whole insane day. "I'm the best man."

She shook her head and whistled. "Man, you are strong. If I were you I either would have punched someone by now, or I'd be curled in a ball in the corner singing show tunes."

"Show tunes?" I asked.

"I find them oddly comforting," she replied. "Don't tell anyone."

Somehow, a laugh escaped my lips. Biff got up and took the dress from me. "Here. Let me help you."

"Thanks."

I quickly unbuttoned my flannel shirt (which I'd worn at Marni's suggestion so that when I took it off it wouldn't ruin my hair and makeup) and stepped out of my jeans. Biff held the dress open on the floor for me to step into, which I did, bracing my hand against her shoulder. I pushed my feet into my black flats as Biff zipped me up.

"Well, I'll tell you one thing," Biff said as we both checked out my reflection in the huge mirror. "This Tommy kid is going to eat his words."

I smiled sadly. "No, he won't. He would never. It's not in his nature to admit he was wrong."

"Is he allergic to anything? Maybe we could sneak it into his meal," she suggested. "By the end of the night we could have him broken out in boils."

I laughed again and the door behind us opened. Mrs. Shay stuck her sleek blond head in.

"Are you two ready? We're doing pictures," she said.

Biff caught my eye in the mirror. "Just try to keep that smile on," she told me. "This is going to be a long day."

"I'll try," I replied.

Mrs. Shay held the door open for us and waved her arm to usher us through. My mother nearly dropped her champagne glass when she saw me.

"Oh my goodness, Farrah! It's like a dream," she said, covering her mouth with her hand.

Is it wrong that her reaction made me want to rip the dress right off my body and tear it into shreds?

"There's the best man!" Marni announced, bringing my entrance to everyone's attention. The rest of the girls fell silent and Calista sneered as she looked me up and down.

"Farrah," Marni crossed the room, the train on her classic A-line dress swishing behind her. Her hair was back in a perfect bun and huge diamond studs twinkled in her ears. "You look absolutely stunning."

"Thanks," I said, willingly falling into the hug she offered. "Then why is Calista looking at me like that?" I whispered into her ear.

"Sheer jealousy," she whispered back.

I took a deep breath. "Right."

She leaned back and smiled at me, touching one of the curls the stylist had left to cascade around my face.

"I really love the dress, Marni," I said. "It's totally perfect. Thank you for picking it."

"Well, that's what sisters are for," she said, lifting her tiny shoulders.

I grinned as more tears filled my eyes. I swear in all my life I had not almost-cried nearly as much as I had the last few days.

"Hey! Helmut! Can I get a picture with the best man over here?" Marni asked, waving to the photographer. He lifted his state-of-the-art camera and hustled over, a look of excitement on his round face.

"What lovely girls you are," he said admiringly as he held up the camera.

"We know," Marni joked.

She put her arm around my waist, so I did the same. Smiling for the camera was a lot more difficult than smiling over Biff's jokes or Marni's sweetness. As the shutter clicked, I forced myself to think of good things. Of my new friends, of the fact that I'd grown to like Marni so much over the past week and a half. I tried. But before long the memory of Connor's devastated face that morning flooded my mind. And Tommy McNabb's obnoxious smirk. And my mother's proud smile as she announced that she'd saved me from a fate worse than death—being dateless.

And then I heard my mother chatting with Mrs. Shay in the corner.

"I know. She looks beautiful, doesn't she?" she said. "Wait until you see her date. This boy is so handsome, Jeanette. I swear, if I could just get these two together for good it would make me a happy woman."

Let's just say I hoped Helmut got some good, smiley photos before I heard *that*.

"Hold it together," Biff said under her breath as Helmut finished up. He and Marni went off to take some pictures with the moms and I leaned back against one of the couches, feeling weak in the knees.

"Did you hear her? Did you hear what she just said?" I asked, shaking with anger.

"Yeah, well, she's delusional," Biff replied.

"I can't take this. I can't hang out with him all day and act like I'm so happy to be his date. I'm going to hurl, I swear," I said.

"So why don't you just tell her?" Biff suggested, growing frustrated. "Tell her what an evil bastard the kid is. You've gotta stick up for yourself, Farrah."

God, that thought was appealing. Or at least it would be, if I had any sense that my mother would remotely believe me. I didn't know what would be more shocking and hard to swallow for her, the idea that Tommy and I had already hooked up without her help, or the notion that Tommy wasn't as perfect as she and the rest of the world had always believed.

"I can't," I said sadly. "We'll get into a fight and I can't do that. Not to Jonah and Marni. Not today."

Biff blew out a sigh. "Well, you're a better woman than I am."

I leaned my head on her shoulder and she threw her arm around me. "I really don't think that's possible," I told her.

She gave me a squeeze and for that moment,

at least, I felt comforted and almost okay. Almost like as long as Biff was around, I could maybe get through this horrific day.

I had never stood still for so long in my entire life. After photos with the female half of the bridal party, my mother and I were excused to go downstairs and take Janssen/Morris family photos with Jonah and Jim and the boys. These were being posed in front of the Christmas trees in the lobby and just being there put me on edge. It was like returning to the scene of the crime. I kept expecting to see Connor and wishing like crazy that I could somehow find a second to grab him and explain. But while some curious bystanders gathered around to watch the proceedings, there was no sight of Connor. He was probably purposely avoiding me. He'd probably do that for the rest of his life. God, that thought was depressing.

Soon, however, I was distracted from my misery. Pictures with the family were total bedlam. Trying to get Hunter and Ben to stand still was a nightmare on a normal day, but today they knew something big was going on, which made them even more hyper than usual. Plus they were dressed up in mini tuxedoes, various parts of which they were shedding at any given moment. I refastened their ties at least thirty times, retied their shoes about a dozen, and once retrieved a tiny jacket from the top of a holly plant where it was flung. By the time the family pics were over, I thought my mother was going to need a Valium.

"All right! Let's get the groom with his groomsmen," Helmut suggested. He turned around and popped what appeared to be an antacid. Apparently the boys had gotten to him, too.

Jonah and I stood in front of the Christmas trees in the lobby as David, Nicholas, and Seth crowded in around us. These guys, at least, were on their best behavior. For once. Maybe they were all still hung over from the night before.

"So, it's the big day!" Jonah said to me, clapping his hands together.

"Sure is," I said, trying to infuse myself with some enthusiasm. "How are you feeling?" I asked Jonah as Helmut positioned us, turning my shoulders to the side and inching Jonah's right foot out a bit.

"I'm okay," he said. "My mouth's a little dry and I'm nervous, but I'll live."

"You seemed pretty wasted last night," I mentioned.

"You think that's Jonah wasted?" David joked. "You clearly haven't let her see the worst of you."

"Thank you for that," I said to Jonah.

"Anytime," he replied.

"Okay, and smile!" Helmut called out.

We did, and he snapped a few photos. Then he took a couple of Jonah with his buddies, which allowed me to sit and rest my legs for a full two minutes. While I was resting, I saw Tommy and his parents stroll into the lobby from the elevators. The very sight of him made my stomach turn. He was looking all *Esquire*-worthy in a sleek tuxedo with a long gray tie. At first I hoped they were just walking through on their way for coffee or something, but they came right over to us and started chatting with my mother. Before I knew it, Tommy was standing right in front of me. My face prickled with heat as I stared past his hip.

"Wow. Look at you," he said. "My mom told me you were wearing a dress, but I didn't believe it."

I scoffed and glared up at him. He gave me a look like *Oh! What are you gonna do?*

"Farrah! We need you, sweetheart," Helmut said, interrupting my rage.

I stood up, forcing Tommy to take a step back. "You're a jackass," I said under my breath.

Tommy laughed and I brushed by him. Jonah stood alone now in front of the twinkling Christmas trees. He took one look at my face, then glanced over at Tommy.

"What's the matter?" he said, placing his hand on my back as I joined him. "Do I need to kick Tommy McNabb's ass?"

"If you weren't getting married in an hour, I'd say go for it," I told him through my teeth.

"Okay, you two! Smile! You love each other! You're brother and sister," Helmut announced, wielding his camera.

"We are? Who knew?" Jonah joked, putting his arm around me.

"Yeah, I don't know if I love you. That might be kind of a stretch," I joked back.

We continued teasing in that vein until the pictures were over and, as a result, I actually smiled some real smiles. Jonah could always bring out the best in me.

"All right! We're all set!" Helmut announced.

"Thank God," I said under my breath.

"Wait, wait, wait!" my mother cried, taking a few steps forward. "Would you mind getting a few of Farrah and her date?"

All the blood drained right out of my face. Tommy, ever compliant to the wishes of parents, stepped forward, smoothing his tie.

"Mom. I really don't think that's necessary," Jonah said, noting my lack of color.

"Jonah, it will only take a moment," my mother

said. "It's not every day that your sister has a date."

Oh. No. She. Didn't. She did *not* just say that at full volume.

A few of the onlookers chuckled and I felt my heart closing up. If there was any chance of me possibly getting through this, I was going to have to shut down and pretend I was somewhere else.

"It's okay," I heard myself say to Jonah.

I backed up toward the trees, and Tommy stood next to me. My mother came flitting over to fuss with my hair, adjust something on my skirt, and touch some kind of pad to my nose. She looked at me proudly before scurrying away again, apparently not noticing the dead look in my eye.

"Put your arm around her, for goodness' sake!" Tommy's mother commented.

Tommy did as he was told and pulled me into him. Helmut started to snap away. Just then—just as I was trying my hardest to put on a smile and get this thing over with as quickly as possible—Connor strode in on the tail of one of his coworkers, nodding as he took some direction from the older man. He paused when he noticed the wedding party and looked straight at me and Tommy. The moment he saw me, his eyes clouded over. He looked right at me, as if he didn't even know me, and then he was gone.

I felt completely weak and empty. I felt like I could just collapse to the floor and cry.

"You smell pretty good, Morris," Tommy whispered in my ear. "Maybe if none of the other bridesmaids are hot we can get to second base tonight."

"Get away from me," I said through my teeth. I was shaking from my head all the way down to my toes.

Tommy laughed and gripped me harder. "You're such a tease."

That was it. Something snapped. Before I knew what I was doing, I had shoved him away with both hands. "Get the hell off of me!"

Tommy tripped sideways. A few people gasped. I turned around and grabbed my mother's wrist, dragging her over toward the wall. She protested the whole way, but I didn't even register what she was saying. It would have been difficult to hear her through all the hyperventilating anyway.

"Farrah! What is wrong with you?" she snapped, clutching my chin between her thumb and forefinger.

"Mom, just shut up and listen to me," I said, removing her hand.

"Farrah! How dare you speak to me—"

"Mom!" I practically yelled.

Jonah was suddenly at my side. "Farrah, what the heck is going on?"

"How could you do this to me, Mom?" I asked, tears in my eyes. "I told you not to fly in a date for me, but you did it anyway. And Tommy McNabb? How could you?"

"Farrah, I don't know what has gotten into you, but you're embarrassing me and yourself," she said. "Tommy McNabb is a dream date. Any girl would be lucky to have him. Especially you."

"He said I was practically a guy," I blurted, glaring at her.

"Excuse me?" she said.

"Junior year." I crossed my arms over my chest. "We were at this party and we started . . . kissing. And we ended up kissing for a really long time and I thought . . ." I took a deep breath and composed myself. "I thought he wanted to be my boyfriend. But when I said that to him, he laughed in my face."

"What?" Jonah said quietly.

"He laughed in my face, Mom. He told me he couldn't date me . . . . He couldn't be seen with me . . . because I was practically a guy."

My mother stared at me in complete shock, her eyes searching mine as if looking for some vestige of sanity. It was exactly as I thought it would be.

She didn't believe me at all. I could read it all over her face. She thought I'd lost my mind.

Jonah, however, turned right around, shoved a couple of bystanders aside, and before Tommy could even react, slammed his fist right across Devil-Spawn's jaw.

"Jonah!" Tommy's mother cried, flying forward.

Tommy hit the ground like a house of cards, and Jonah stood over him. "You stay the hell away from my sister."

In front of me, my mother cleared her throat and straightened the beaded jacket on her mother-of-the-groom dress. She smoothed her hair and strode right over to Tommy's parents, to apologize for my brother's behavior, I presume. I leaned back against the wall and tried to breathe. This was a nightmare. A total nightmare.

"Susan, Trevor, thank you for bringing Tommy all this way," my mother said as Tommy's dad helped him off the floor. "You are both still welcome to attend the wedding. Your son, however, is not."

"What?" Tommy blurted. "I gave up the Hamptons for this shit!"

"Yes, well, behavior like yours would have fit

right in there, I'm sure," my mother said coolly, looking down her nose at him. "But nobody treats my daughter that way."

"I can't believe you did that," I said as my mother and I walked toward the atrium for the ceremony. She was clutching my hand, as she had been ever since telling off the McNabbs. "I really can't believe you did that."

"Neither can I," she replied, wide-eyed. She actually looked invigorated by what she'd done. Almost younger. Maybe defiance was better than Botox. "Farrah, why did you never tell me about this?" she asked, pausing to let the rest of the bridal party go by.

I felt my throat thicken and I looked at the floor. "Honestly?"

"Honesty would be good," she replied.

I swallowed hard. "I kind of thought you'd agree with him."

"What?!" she asked. Her hand flew to her chest and she looked stunned.

"Are you really that surprised, Mom?" I said. "Ever since I was a little kid you've been trying to change me. You tried to make me take ballet, you put me in the Brownies, you were always buying me all those skirts and dresses when I was never going to wear them. I know you always wished I was a cheerleader instead of a track star. I figured . . . I figured you'd get where Tommy was coming from, and I just didn't want to hear that."

My mother's eyes welled with tears as she looked at me. She reached up and touched my cheek with her hand, pressing her lips together.

"Oh, honey. I'm so sorry," she said. "I thought it was all my fault. I thought I left you alone with your brother so much when you were small that I had turned you into a tomboy and I was just trying to, I don't know, balance it out. I didn't want you to miss out on anything because I wasn't there for you."

"Well, maybe that *is* part of the reason I'm a tomboy, but I like being a tomboy. I'm balanced. Really," I told her.

"And beautiful," she said with a smile.

I laughed and took a step back, swishing the skirt of my dress back and forth. "I know, right? I clean up good, don't I?"

My mother nodded proudly. "You sure do."

"Five minutes until we start the processional!" Marni's mother told us as she hurried by. Biff was right behind her and she paused and grabbed my arm.

"Can I borrow her for a second, Mrs. Janssen?" she asked.

"Sure. I'll be right inside," Mom told me. "We'll talk more later."

"Okay," I replied. She blew me a kiss and walked into the sun-drenched atrium. That was when I noticed the death grip Biff had on my arm. "Ow! What?" I asked her, yanking myself away.

"I found Connor. He's in the bridal room setting it up for after the ceremony, and he's alone," she whispered.

My heart thumped extra hard. "So?"

"So now's your chance. Go in there and explain!"

"But your mom said we only have five minutes," I protested.

"That's twenty in wedding speak. Haven't you ever been in one of these things before?" she asked. "Now go!"

She turned me around and shoved me down the hall. My heart pounding, I made my way toward the end until I found the door marked BRIDAL SUITE. I stood there for a moment and told myself that if I could stand up to Tommy McNabb, I could do this. If I could tell my mother how I felt, I could do this. Then I took a deep breath and opened the door.

"Hi."

Connor looked up from the plate of chocolate-covered strawberries he was arranging. His expression was unreadable.

"You're not supposed to be in here," he said. "It's bride and groom only."

Well. That was more readable.

"I know, but Connor, you have to let me explain," I said. I sounded desperate, and hated it, but what could I do? I *was* desperate. The last thing in the world I wanted was to lose him. I knew I had screwed up, but if he cared about me, he'd have to hear me out. Wouldn't he?

"What's to explain?" He continued to fuss around the room, placing a bottle of champagne on ice, fluffing the throw pillows on the couch. "You lied. You lied about who you are, why you're here, what you do. You even lied about your name."

"Not really. I've been going by Jane ever since September," I reminded him. "Everybody at school knows me as Jane."

He stood up straight. "Right! So you've been lying to everyone, not just me. That makes me feel much better."

Ouch. That one hurt.

"Connor, please—"

He touched the earpiece in his ear and flipped a switch on the little black box on his belt. "Yeah, Todd, I'll be right there," he said. "Sorry," he told me flatly. "Some of us have to work for a living."

Then he strode right past me and out the door.

Chapter 16

Thank you, Jonah, for making me the best man instead of a bridesmaid. As the best man, I got to hang out with him in the small waiting room just off the altar space. I got to just step out into place instead of walking down the long white aisle, where hundreds of people would be watching me. Considering everything that had happened that morning, I didn't trust myself not to get distracted and walk into one of the guests, or trip on my hem, or do something equally embarrassing. As all those celebutantes and trust-fund babies and international millionaires gathered under the domed glass ceiling of the atrium, Jonah and I chilled in the side room, thumb-wrestling. The other guys would have been there as well, but they couldn't keep themselves from hanging by the wall inside and taking stock of all the starlets in the room. Jonah had given them his blessing to do so once their constant opening of the door to survey the situation had started to drive him bonkers.

"Dude! I've beaten you four out of five," Jonah said as I tried to hook my thumb around his. "Surrender, already."

"Never!"

Of course, the second the string quartet started to play, he froze and I pinned him easy.

"Yes! You suck!" I whisper-taunted. I was trying to get into the spirit of things. This was, after all, his day. Even if my heart had quite recently been broken.

Jonah looked at the door and picked up his tuxedo jacket. I could practically feel his heart beating. It took over the entire room.

"Last chance to bail," I joked. "I promise I'll stall them so you can get a head start."

"Ha-ha," he replied. I watched his Adam's apple bob up and down and grabbed him a bottle of water out of the mini fridge. "Thanks," he said, after taking a long drink.

The door opened and Emily, dressed in a tasteful black gown, stuck her head in.

"You're on," she said with a smile.

Jonah nodded. "Let's do this."

I helped him slip his arms into his jacket, straightened his tie, and slapped him once on the shoulder.

"Good luck out there, buddy," I said.

"Thanks for being here, Farrah," he replied.

I lifted my shoulders. "Where else would I be?"

He laughed and, after taking a deep breath, stepped out into the atrium. I grabbed my small bouquet of white roses and followed. Dozens of camera bulbs flashed as we took our places at the front of the room. Hundreds of strangers grinned at us, and my brother reached back to squeeze my hand. My heart swelled and I squeezed back. I knew what he was thinking.

None of these random people matter. I'm glad you're here.

The atrium was a large round room near the back of the hotel, made up entirely of windows. Being that it was the dead of winter, the sun had long since gone down, but all the snowy evergreen trees outside the windows had been decorated with twinkling white lights and shimmering crystal icicles. Inside, the room had been decorated like a fairy wonderland. Garlands of fresh flowers in white and pink were draped from the ceiling and all of the pews. Candles twinkled all around the altar, interspersed with huge flower arrangements. There were rose petals on the floor, on the chairs, on the windowsills, on every available surface. It was incredibly romantic, but for some reason all I could think about was how thousands upon thousands of flowers had made the ultimate sacrifice for Marni's vision.

I chuckled to myself, then giggled some more as I realized that I was still able to feel giddy. I guess weddings trump everything else.

"What?" Jonah said quietly.

"Nothing," I replied. "Just happy for you."

He eyed me suspiciously but said nothing. My mother waved at us from the front row, where she sat with Jim and the boys and my aunt Shari and her latest husband. Then the music changed and the processional started. Every last guest in the room shifted in their seat, the better to see the bridesmaids on their way down the aisle. First came Carina, then Jenna. Then, when Calista stepped out onto the white carpet, the place went crazy with flashing and clicking. Calista shook her hair back and lifted her chin as she strode down the aisle, milking every minute of it. I could just imagine how many magazines were going to have front-page shots of her the following week. My brother's wedding, on the cover of *Us Weekly*. That is just too bizarre. She made it to the front and still the cameras continued to flash. I had to close my eyes to keep from getting blinded. Then Biff stepped through the doors. She walked slowly, purposefully to the front, mouthed "hi" to me and my brother, then stopped and faced the back of the guests.

Once again, the music changed. The classic wedding march began, and Marni and her parents stepped into view. There were a few awed gasps and everyone in the atrium stood.

"This is it," I said through my teeth.

"Shut up," Jonah replied.

I grinned, my heart fluttering around in excitement. This was actually kind of fun.

Marni was extremely poised and tear-free as she made her way down the aisle, nodding to friends and family. Helmut backed down the aisle in front of her, snapping about a zillion close-up pictures as the other photogs kept to the walls and did the best they could. When she arrived at the end of the aisle she kissed both her parents, then took Jonah's arm. I took one look at the perfectly content, excited, loving look on his face, and a tear spilled down my cheek.

My brother was truly happy. And I was pleased to discover that I was truly happy for him.

For the next two hours I kept my eyes peeled for Connor. During post-ceremony pictures, a few waiters came in and out with champagne and fruit platters, but he was not among them. Then, at the

cocktail hour, there were dozens of people in tuxedoes serving hors d'oeuvres and drinks, but again,
no sign of him. Still, every time I saw the River
Lodge's tailed tuxedoes, my heart lurched. It made
for a very alarming and uncomfortable evening. I
had to do something to distract myself.

So I ate way too much. So much that I started
to wonder if I was, perhaps, an emotional eater.
But I felt better and less gluttonous when I realized
that everyone around me was doing the same. No
one could avoid it. The food was that exquisite.
The cocktail hour was in a huge room with ten different stations from sushi to pasta to Carnegie Deli
to Thai to western favorites like chicken-fried steak
and beans—plus the passed hors d'oeuvres. By the
time that was over, I was already stuffed. Then we
were ushered into the ballroom by an army of
tuxedoed waiters and hostesses and another round
of food began. Salad course, cheese course, pasta
course. It was out of control. It wasn't until I had
polished off my penne vodka that Biff reminded
me we still had to make our speeches. Soon.

Then, of course, I regretted every last bite I had
taken.

I looked up from my chair at the head table
and took in the hundreds and hundreds of faces.
Everyone was eating, laughing, sipping their

drinks. Candlelight flickered all over the room, twinkling in the reflection from the champagne flutes and silver platters. They all seemed very far away, all happy and relaxed and ready to party. Not nervous at all. It was as if we weren't even existing on the same plane.

Suddenly, with a swish of organza, Emily appeared at the end of the table with a microphone. I gulped at the sight of it.

"All right, ladies. Speech time," she whispered. "Who wants to go first?"

"I will!" Biff volunteered.

I was startled by her enthusiasm, but when she grabbed the mike, I didn't protest. Let her throw herself to the wolves first. At least it would give me more time to mentally prepare.

"Don't be nervous," Jonah whispered to me as Biff stood up. "It's only the most important speech you'll ever make in your life and I'll hate you forever if you embarrass me."

He grinned and I wanted to rip his head off right then and there. "You know sometimes, Jonah, your sense of humor is not an asset," I told him.

He simply took a sip of his water and crunched some ice in response.

"Jerk," I said under my breath. But, of course,

his teasing had the desired effect. My blood was racing so fast through my veins I was certain I was going to burst a vessel. I reached for my purse, pulled out the note card with my speech on it, and tried to pay attention to Biff.

"Hello, everyone," she said into the microphone. "If I could have your attention, please, we can get this painful ritual over with."

There were a few chuckles throughout the room and it fell completely silent. Unreal. She had them in the palm of her hand with one sentence.

"Many of you know me, but for those of you who don't, I'm Buffy Shay, Marni's unfortunately named younger sister."

More laughter. My speech crumpled in my sweaty palm.

"Those of you who do know me, know that I'm not big with the public displays, so I'm going to keep this short," Biff continued.

I took a deep breath to try to calm my heart. Out of the corner of my eye, I saw one of the ballroom doors silently open, and Connor stepped through. My stomach dropped right out of my body at the sight of him. Why had he chosen *this* moment to show up? He stepped along the wall, unobtrusive, and whispered some kind of direction to one of the waiters. Then he looked up—looked straight at me—and held my gaze for a long, long moment. I couldn't breathe to save my life. I would have given anything on this planet to know, in that moment, what he was thinking.

"I love you, Marni. And you, too, Jonah. But if you don't take care of my sister, I will hunt you down and go all vampire slayer on your ass. I do, after all, have the name."

Jonah cracked up laughing and suddenly everyone was applauding. Biff slipped behind my chair to hug Jonah and Marni. She was already done. She was handing me the microphone. How had this happened? Where had my prep time gone?

I stared at the mike, clutched in my sweaty fingers. There were no words in my mind other than *Connor*. He was still there. Still watching. And so was everyone else in the room.

"Farrah. You're on," Jonah whispered.

I couldn't move. I couldn't. Biff took the microphone again and spoke into it. "And now, the best . . . *girl* . . . Farrah Morris!" There was more applause and Biff practically yanked me out of my chair. She placed the microphone in my cold hand and whispered in my ear. "You can do this. You know what you're going to say and in two minutes it'll all be over. Just go for it."

I nodded, feeling sweaty and floaty and not at

all focused, and turned toward the room.

"Hi . . . hi, everyone. I'm—"

"We can't hear you!" someone yelled from the back of the room.

"Oh. Sorry." I lifted the microphone to my mouth and spoke again. "I'm Farrah Morris."

My words boomed out of the hidden speakers and everyone in the room groaned. Emily stepped forward and pulled my hand down, then smiled encouragingly. I glanced at the doors, envisioning my escape. But then Jonah reached out and squeezed my free hand and I knew I wasn't going anywhere. I just had to get through this. I glanced at my crumpled note card.

"I'm Farrah Morris and I'm Jonah's little sister. I was surprised when he asked me to be his best man, being that I'm the wrong gender and all—"

There were a few laughs and that buoyed me a bit.

"But then I realized that it made perfect sense. Because while Jonah and I both have some good friends in this world, we've always been each other's best friend. We never had what you would call a normal brother-sister relationship. Because when our dad, Frederick Morris, got sick when we were very young, we ended up spending a lot of time together. During those times my brother taught me how to tie my shoes, how to fish, how to catch frogs and lightning bugs, how to hit a baseball, and which was the coolest Star Wars movie."

"The Empire Strikes Back!" Nicholas announced.

"That's right!" Jonah said.

That time even I laughed, and I relaxed even more.

"I don't know if I turned out to be a tomboy because of the influence my brother had on me, or if I would have found that path on my own, but I like who I've become, and I give him a lot of credit for making me the person I am today. And even though we're all grown-up now, my brother's still teaching me things every day. Just recently, watching him and Marni together, I've learned what it is to find true love. I've learned how very precious that is. And I've learned that when you find it, you should hold on to it, no matter what obstacles might stand in your way."

As I said this, my eyes found Connor's in the crowd. He gazed back at me, and it might have just been all the candlelight that separated us, but I could have sworn his eyes were softening.

"I know that I'm not perfect. None of us are. We all make mistakes and do crazy things when we're scared, but if love is the motivation for those crazy things," I said, my heart pounding painfully, "then I think that, just maybe, people should over- look them. And, you know, give other people a second chance."

"Uh, Farrah?" Biff whispered. "I think you're getting a bit off topic."

I blinked. "Oh, right. Sorry." I glanced down at my notes and cleared my throat. "Anyway, Jonah, Marni, I want you guys to know how much I look up to both of you. The way you are together, it's just something I never thought actually existed in real life. And I just think that's really cool."

Marni clucked her tongue and smiled, her eyes swimming. Jonah shook his head at me, but in a good way.

"So let's all raise our glasses," I said, dropping my speech and lifting my champagne flute. "To Marni and Jonah and to finding true love!"

"To true love!" a few people shouted in response.

Everyone sipped their champagne, then applauded my semi–non sequitur efforts. My brother got up and hugged me so hard I actually coughed.

"That was awesome, Farrah," he said. "Thank you."

A couple of tears spilled over and I wiped them

quickly away. "You're welcome, jerk," I replied, punching his arm.

Marni hugged me as well, while Helmut snapped a few pictures. When we parted, I glanced at Connor again. He hadn't moved, and he still wore that serious expression. I willed him to come over to me. To stride across the room, take me in his arms, and kiss me. To tell me that he'd heard and understood every word I said and that he forgave every indiscretion of the past two weeks.

He stared into my eyes from across the room for a long, agonizing, and exciting moment. Then he looked down at his shoes, turned on his heel, and was gone.

I dropped down into my chair as the music started to pump up and hundreds of people flooded the dance floor.

"Are you okay?" Biff asked me, touching my arm.

"I guess it's really over," I said, hardly able to comprehend it myself. "I think he really hates me."

For the rest of the night I forced myself to at least appear as if I was having fun. I danced to a couple of fast songs, stepping from side to side and pushing a smile onto my face whenever I felt my mother, Jonah, or Marni looking at me. I made a reasonable attempt at a laugh when Marni mashed a hunk of cake into Jonah's face during the cake-cutting ceremony. I even got on the dance floor when Marni went to throw her bouquet, but quickly moved toward the back of the pack when no one was looking. Good thing, too. Carina gave Calista a black eye with her elbow as she lunged for it. Guess someone was finally ready to step out of Calista's sizable shadow.

Of course, every chance I could, I retreated to my chair at the head table to wallow. At any given moment, there were about a million thoughts and emotions swirling through me and it was starting to make me dizzy. I was indescribably sad. For the past few days I had been walking on air, high on my relationship with my first real boyfriend, and now, it appeared, that was entirely over. Over before it really had a chance to get off the ground. I was crushed that Connor had, in the course of one day, turned his back on me three full times. Clearly I didn't mean that much to him, if he wouldn't even hear me out. If my heartfelt speech didn't touch him even one iota. I guess I didn't mean as much to him as he meant to me . . . which just made me angry. I mean, okay, I knew what I had done was wrong. But he was wrong, too, to not let me explain. It was, after all, his own prejudice against the wealthy that had forced me to lie about who I was in the first place. And when you thought about it, it wasn't even me who had lied. It was Biff. I'd just gone along with it. I was malleable and weak, maybe, but not evil and spiteful. Wasn't he just a huge jerk to not see that?

At this point in my logic, I would get exhausted and slump down farther in my chair until my mother came along to tell me to sit up or Biff would pull me out to dance. And that was how my night plodded along, each hour passing in a blur of self-pity, self-righteousness, and bad dancing, until that fateful moment finally arrived.

"Ladies and gentlemen, in just a few moments, we'll be starting the countdown to the new year!" the bandleader announced.

Excited whispers fluttered throughout the room, causing a stir in many a heart, I supposed. I, myself, slumped back against the nearest wall. On the screen behind the bandstand, which had been playing a slide show of old family pictures of Jonah and Marni all night, a countdown from one minute appeared.

"If you're going to be kissing anyone at midnight, better grab that person now," the bandleader suggested happily.

Could this possibly be any more torturous? I

thought. Even as, somewhere in the back of my mind, I wondered if *this* was it. Was this the romantic moment I'd been secretly hoping for all night? Was Connor just waiting for midnight to come in and lay a big kiss on me and tell me everything was going to be all right? I kind of doubted it, but as the clock wound down to thirty seconds, I straightened up anyway.

Everyone was gathering in the center of the dance floor. As skirts swished and champagne glasses clinked, Biff, Nicholas, and David made their way over to me.

"So, Little Red. Got someone to kiss?" David asked me.

I felt like someone had just punched me in the stomach. "No. You?"

"No," he said. "Nicholas is gonna kiss Biff."

"You are?" I asked.

"They flipped a coin for me," Biff commented, lifting one shoulder before downing the rest of her champagne. She hiccuped and slapped the glass down on the table. "I figured what the heck."

"They flipped for you, huh?" I said. "Wow, guys. That's very romantic."

"Yeah, well. You gotta do what you gotta do," Nicholas told me with a wink.

"So, wanna kiss me, then?" David asked,

265

nudging me with his arm.

Even in my seriously deadened state, that proposition perked me up a bit. But then I realized that if Connor *did* happen to choose the stroke of midnight to make his grand entrance and forgive me, his plans would most definitely change if he saw me kissing another guy.

"I can't. I'm sorry," I said, biting my lip.

"You're kidding," David replied. "You're turning *me* down?"

"As insane as it sounds, yeah," I joked back. "I'm sort of hoping my Prince Charming will swoop in."

"Well, he better swoop soon," Nicholas said. "Cuz here we go."

I glanced up at the ticking clock just as everyone around me started shouting.

"Ten! Nine! Eight!"

I glanced around the room from tuxedoed waiter to tuxedoed waitress. Connor wasn't there.

"Seven! Six! Five!"

"Crap," David said. "I can't *not* kiss someone at midnight. That is just so wrong."

"Four! Three! Two!"

Come on, Connor. Come on . . .

"One! Happy New Year!" Nicholas grabbed Biff, dipped her back, and kissed her as her eyes widened in surprise. David grabbed the hand of the first girl who walked past him, which happened to be Carina, spun her around, and laid one on her as she clutched the bridal bouquet at her side. In the center of the dance floor, the bride and groom kissed under a spotlight just as confetti and rose petals and balloons rained down from the ceiling.

Everyone cheered and applauded and walked around, giving and getting more smooches. But no one reached for my hand. No one dipped me or surprised me or went anywhere near my lonely lips. And at that moment, I decided I had done enough pretending for one night. I'd done enough of everything. I quietly slipped away from Biff and the others and slunk off for the solitude of my room.

Chapter 17

"You should totally come to Paris with me," Biff said the next day as we stood outside her waiting limo. We had said good-bye to Jonah and Marni that morning and now it was time to say good-bye to each other. A light snow dusted our coats and hair as wind swirled in the trees. "Do you even comprehend the quality of the pastries they have there?"

I laughed and shook my head. Her driver hoisted Biff's hot-pink-and-lime-green luggage into the trunk. The terry cloth belt, from what was clearly one of the River Lodge's exclusive robes, stuck out of one of them, and he quickly tucked it inside and zipped up the bag. He looked up at me and winked. Guess the guys that worked here didn't mind when the guests pilfered stuff from the rooms.

"I wish I could, but I have to go back to school in a few days," I told her. "They put out this double-size issue of the school paper to welcome everyone back and I have to work on it."

"You are way too responsible for your own good," she said.

"What about you? When do you have to be back at school?" I asked.

She shrugged. "I wrote it down somewhere. I'm sure they won't miss me if I'm a few days late."

The driver slammed the trunk and came around the side of the car. "We should get going, Miss," he said, touching the brim of his hat. "Your parents' car left half an hour ago."

"Okay. Just waiting for something," Biff said, looking past me. Her eyes lit up and she waved. "Here it is."

I turned and saw one of the bellboys walking over to us with two big pink pastry boxes. He handed them to Biff and she slipped him a bill. Even if she was the rebel of the family, she certainly was down with their customs. She placed one of the boxes into the car, then handed the other to me.

"It's a chocolate cake to remember me by," she said. "Don't share it with anyone, least of all the psycho twins. I don't even want to know the havoc they'd wreak on that much sugar."

I laughed. I could actually smell the chocolaty goodness through the box. "I promise."

Biff's eyes grew serious. "You know, when I was in there ordering the cake I saw Connor."

My heart skipped a beat. "I don't want to talk about him."

"Well, if it makes you feel any better, he looked miserable," she said.

"Probably because all the big tippers are leaving," I joked. She stared at me and I stared at the ground. "He doesn't want to have anything to do with me, Biff. It's pointless to even talk about it."

"You've got a lot to learn about guys, *Jane*," Biff said.

"What do you mean?"

"Lesson number one: A guy doesn't walk around looking that miserable if he wants nothing to do with you."

I felt a flutter of hope. "You think?"

"Call me when he comes to his senses," she told me, slipping her sunglasses on. "I'll be waiting."

She leaned forward and gave me a tight squeeze, then jumped into the car. I waved as the limo pulled away. When it got to the bottom of the drive, she rolled down the window and stuck out her hand, already clutching a hunk of cake. I laughed, relishing the bittersweetness of the moment, then hugged my cake box to me and walked back inside.

I had one last dinner with my mom, Jim, and the boys before sending them off in a car for the airport. The Shays had gotten all of us a late checkout, so I packed my bags slowly before calling for the bellhop. Every second I wished to hear a knock on my door. Wished that Connor would show up with another apology and another bouquet. Or just show up so that I could explain everything. But he never came.

Finally, when it was dark as pitch outside and everything was long since folded away and zipped up, I knew I was being silly and I couldn't put it off any longer. I made the call and headed downstairs.

"The car will be here in about ten minutes, Miss," the bellman told me as we stood in the center of the gleaming lobby.

I glanced toward the back of the hotel and the balcony overlooking the trees where Connor and I had spent our Christmas together. I don't know if I was feeling nostalgic or masochistic—maybe a little bit of both—when I heard myself say, "I'm going to wait out there, if you don't mind."

He smiled. "I'll come get you when your ride arrives."

"Thanks."

I wandered slowly, past the fireplace and all the cozy, chatting guests, out into the cold. The wind had kicked up a bit since that morning and the balcony was deserted. More than fine by me. Alone seemed like a good state to be in at that moment. I pulled my hat down over my ears and leaned on the railing, looking out at the trees. I couldn't believe how much had changed in just a few days. How much I'd lost. The last time I had been out here I'd been so happy and warm and hopeful and now . . . now I was just—

"There she is again, looking all serious."

My heart stopped and I turned around. Connor stood behind me, his hands in the pockets of his coat. He looked incredible. His stubble was growing back and he wore a green wool hat that brought out his eyes.

"What are you doing here?" I asked him.

"I was hoping to catch you before you left."

My mind reeled. I couldn't believe he actually wanted to see me. Was I hallucinating from the cold? He took a few steps toward me until I could smell that particular clean, woodsy scent of his and I knew he was real.

"I had to ask you," he said. "Did you mean everything you said last night? In your speech?"

"Yeah," I replied. "Every word."

He studied my face, and I wasn't sure if he was going to talk again, but I couldn't waste this chance. I had to tell him what I'd been thinking. I had to finally explain.

"Connor, all I've wanted from the first time I saw you was to be with you," I told him. "And that night in the kitchen, it seemed like you wouldn't want to know me if you knew who I really was. Then Biff made up that nanny story and I just . . . I went along with it. I know it wasn't right, but you seemed to hate all the wedding people so much and I didn't want to take that chance. I—"

"You don't have to explain," he said, lifting a hand. "The whole thing was just stupid, right from the start. When I think about how I mocked those people. How dumb I must have sounded . . . and they were your friends—your family." He covered his face with his hands for a moment like he wished he could block the memory. "I feel like such an idiot."

"*You* feel like an idiot? I'm the one who lied," I told him.

"Well, yeah. But I can understand why when I remember the things I said," he told me. "I spent the whole day trying to figure out how to apologize, but nothing sounded good enough, so I just came here hoping you hadn't left yet and—"

"Here I am," I said with a smile.

He smiled back. "Here you are."

Just then, the wind blasted by us, throwing me right into Connor's arms. I clutched at the sleeves of his coat and we both laughed.

"I don't think the universe is going to let us stay very far away from each other," he said, holding on to me.

"I guess not," I replied.

"So you didn't keep me a secret because you were ashamed to be dating lowly concierge guy? You weren't ashamed of me?" he asked.

"What? No! It was way more complicated than that. But that is so not me," I said.

"Then who are you, exactly? Jane, the intrepid reporter-slash-tomboy, or Farrah, the socialite daughter-slash-best man?"

I sighed and looked up at him. "A little bit of both?"

Connor smiled. "Good. Because I love hanging out with Jane, but Farrah looked pretty damn hot in that black dress."

I cracked up laughing and Connor held me closer. Wrapped up in his arms I couldn't feel the wind or the cold. I felt nothing but his warmth and the glee of the impossible having come true.

Connor was holding me again. At that moment I felt like anything could happen.

"I love you, Connor," I heard myself say.

"I love you, too, Farrah," he replied, touching my cheek with his fingertips.

It was the first time in my entire life that I adored hearing my name.

There's more winter romance to come—
might as well get

Snowed In

Turn the page for a sneak peek!

Snowed In

I am so not a morning person. And early morning? Forget it. As far as I'm concerned, it should have never been invented.

I was snuggled in my bed, under a mound of blankets, my head beneath my pillow, trying to ignore the wind shrieking around outside. Because the house was old, it wasn't very well insulated or sealed. Everything seemed to rattle.

I rolled over and sighed. It was still dark and dreary, but my internal clock told me I needed coffee.

Wearing my not-so-sexy flannel trousers and long-sleeved shirt, I clambered out of bed and put on my fuzzy purple slippers. Shivering, I slipped on my thick robe, but didn't bother to tie it. I was going to head quickly down the stairs to the bathroom, where hopefully I could find more warmth, along with my toothbrush and hairbrush.

The stairs did their usual creaking as I hurried down them. Briefly, I stopped to look through the circular window and saw the silhouette of someone trudging along the street. I wondered how long it would take me to get used to all the snow.

When I got to the bottom of the stairs, I turned into the hallway and came up short.

A lumberjack was standing there.

Or at least, that's what he looked like. A really young, really *hot* lumberjack. He was tall and broad, with midnight black hair that curled around his ears and across his brow, creating the perfect frame for his startling blue eyes.

He was wearing an unbuttoned red plaid flannel shirt that was so thick it was almost a jacket. Beneath that he wore a black turtleneck sweater. He was turned slightly so I couldn't see his other hand.

Lumberjacks carried axes. I had a flashback to *The Shining*. My heart hammered against my ribs. I didn't know this guy. Who was he? And where was Mom?

He grinned. "Hey."

"Who are you?" I snapped, jerking the sides of my robe together and tying the sash.

His eyebrows shot up. "Most people I know respond to a greeting with another greeting."

"Well, I'm not someone you know, now, am I? For all I know you're a serial killer."

He chuckled. How could anyone chuckle in the morning?

"Do I look like a serial killer?" he asked.

I guessed not, but still . . .

"What are you doing here?" I demanded.

"Your mom hired my dad to do some repairs. They're in the kitchen discussing details."

"So you just decided to make yourself at home?"

He narrowed his eyes. "Your mom said I could look around. I'm Josh Wynter, by the way."

"And do you become Josh Summer in June?" I asked.

Okay, it was totally lame, a stupid thing to say, but I was still reeling from the fact that a hot guy— were all the guys on this island hot?—was roaming the halls and I was . . .

Not at my best. Ratty robe. Fuzzy slippers. Hair tangled. Teeth unbrushed.

And have I mentioned that I am not a morning person?

"Actually," he said at last, as though finally catching on to my not-so-witty banter, "I stay Josh Wynter all year. Do you stay unfriendly?"

"That does not deserve an answer," I mumbled as I shoved past him as quickly as I could and went into the bathroom. I slammed the door shut.

Okay, I *had* been unfriendly, rude even, but he was so unexpected. And so hot. And I already had a date for Friday night.

What was I supposed to do? Flirt with him? Would that make me the island slut? Nathalie had

4

been dating the same guy for years! Was that how it worked here?

I stayed with my ear pressed to the door until I heard him walk off, down the stairs. At least, it sounded like he was going down to the second floor, but everything echoed around here. What if he was, in fact, on his way *up* to my room?

I wish I'd told him that his "looking around" ended on the third floor. Although based on my behavior, he probably figured that out.

I pressed my back to the door and slid to the floor.

I had overreacted. Totally. He'd scared me. But not in the ax murderer kind of way.

I'd never before felt such an . . . *attraction* to a guy.

That's what I'd been in the hallway just then. Nervous. I'd never been so unsettled around a guy. So why this one?

It didn't make sense. I'd always been cool around guys.

It didn't help matters that when I finally got to my feet and looked in the mirror, I was reminded of my unflattering appearance. I'd given Josh Wynter the worst impression of me in every way imaginable.

Why did I feel such overwhelming disappointment?